SUCCESSION

Quest of Fire

BRETT ARMSTRONG

Expanse Books

Published by Expanse Books,
an imprint of Scrivenings Press LLC
15 Lucky Lane
Morrilton, Arkansas 72110
https://ScriveningsPress.com

Printed in the United States of America

Paperback ISBN 978-1-64917-066-8

eBook ISBN 978-1-64917-067-5

Library of Congress Control Number: 2020946290

Cover by Linda Fulkerson, bookmarketinggraphics.com

This book is dedicated to the glory of God, without Whom there would be no words worth reading and with Whom the darkest paths can be trod with courage.

ACKNOWLEDGMENTS

Without the tireless support of my family I couldn't make it as far as I have. My mom, who has lovingly read everything I've ever written—usually twice—and my dad who always has words of encouragement and is a role model of godliness, my wife who accommodates and assists and inspires my writing daily, and my little boy who fills my days with the happiness and energy it takes to keep going.

I also owe a tremendous debt to Eric Dotseth, the talented artist who inked the artwork in this book and hears out my story ideas with minimal laughter and head shaking.

Erin Howard, Kathy Cretsinger, and Linda Fulkerson; each of whom took a chance on my *Quest of Fire* series and gave it the chance to find its way into readers' hands. I can't begin to express what it means to me to get to share these stories.

Peter Younghusband, who is an incredible encourager and supporter along the storytelling road I'm traveling.

All of the readers who have given my stories a chance and

through their comments, reviews, and continued reading have helped turn my dream of being a novelist into a reality.

Northwestern Lowlands
Hoarcrest
Caldoness
Pepin's Fjord/ Pepin's Folly
Eigh River
Seabridge
Albaron
Caroon River
Glower River
Avon-caroon
Ordumair
Glowerrothes
Wolfglen River
Corcaran River
Isle of Fens
Langlan's Bay
Crystal Cliff
Tawevnen River
Wendelwell
Gerlieu River
Orhal River
Soraby (Aaegen)
Vogteremark
Hildecrest
Molten Rumen
Ermer River
Glastonae
Steepside River
Cuan Cover
Daggernome
Penbrooke
Cherowith
Glaston River
Birschen River
Searsmoor River
Ecthelowall
Greenshard River
Burned Golden Forest
Bay of Bris
Grindale
Bracken
Creston
Free Creek
Glascrest River
Mills River
Estonbury (Estona)
Ecthalon
Narrowville
Lake Earlheld
Lake Norling
Forested March of Cromwell
Fort Valence
Fairwinds (Bonus Mare)
Falconcleft
Middlebane Islands
Merlais
Kinsbane
New Ecthelowall
Castle Letolk
Abaross
Carmine Glades
Isle of Geists
Durky Downs
Tonchford
Ironheld
West Haven
Stormridge
Maple Point
R"resbruck
Libertias
Fell Inlet
Low Birschen River
Middling River
Black River
Port Jarneth
Elenvis
Lone River
Knight's River
Youngsland
Bright Pond
Kirke
Peter's March
Lake Pax

Bay of Bris
Alessia's Inlet
Nighey's Spring
Ermer River
Vogsland Stream
Nighey Copse
Felgash
Bris
Coastal Forest
Amber Steppe
Bradden River
Rush Creek
Estonbury
Fingers of the Bradden
Wither Brook
Stag Pond
Finnel Lakes
Tyarald River
Bracken Forest
Nub Lake
Ulric's Run
Kolde Pond
Nallietrue Forest
Bracken
Grinndale
Merl Hills
Siochail Plains
Wirgerd's Glade
Cupraus
Quick Creek
Jarl's Top
Didymii Peaks
Lake Norling
Slopestead
Perilous Peak
Terstwell Manor
Split Stream
Mount Horth
Starling Falls
Tepid Falls
Riven Hollow
Berry Creek
Sweeny Knob
Doldgek Swamp
Horthpass Forest
Mount Gern
Gern Copper Mines

PART I

OLD WOUNDS

1

Year 1557 of the Middle Era

"I have a bad feeling about this, Father." Meredoch felt a scowl contorting his face.

"I'll bear that in mind. But you really mustn't fret. You're only twelve, so I'm sure this is frightful, but it has been decades since any serious tensions came between the Ords and Ecthels."

His father seemed to sigh for two when Meredoch didn't brighten. Hollowed into Mount Fiorsruthain's side, the narrow room had an annoying echo.

Meredoch's father crossed to stand nearer him. The room was almost too small for the man to rise to his full height. Wearing his most ornate armor, it barely contained him at all. Scents of cinnamon apples from his mother's cooking in the next room only added to Meredoch's discomfort. Their home, one of the more luxurious in the city of Ordumair, offered no place for Meredoch to escape this conversation or its dread.

"Then why do they need you to negotiate for them?" Meredoch fussed with the wool sheets on his bed. A tuft of straw stuck out, and he tucked it back under. He stared up at his father.

If the large man smiled, it was lost in the tangle of his bushy beard. His voice resonated with his continued amusement. "I arbitrate. As Defender of the Realm, I'm impartial and responsible for the peace of all the northlands."

Meredoch crossed his arms over his chest and slumped against the wall of his room. This had all been explained to him before. Except this time involved real danger. Everyone in Ordumair was talking of open war.

Sir Augustine MacCowell rubbed his son's head, mussing his dark, shaggy hair. "You know lad, I have been doing this for quite some time now. Long before you were born, in fact."

"I don't know how you made it this long," Meredoch snapped.

A fit of laughter seized Augustine. Meredoch was even more annoyed. His father should be austere and thoughtful like his best friend Duncoin's father. Not laughing and making light of this. *Who is the child here, anyway?*

Augustine grabbed the boy into his arms and gave him a squeeze. "Well then, thank the Great King, I have you now."

Meredoch wrestled free and tried to keep up his stern front, but it was faltering. His hand slid along the bed and gripped his pillow, ready to strike a sneaky blow.

Rapping on his room's heavy oak door intruded. Though his father tried to mask it, Meredoch could see a somberness come over him.

"Yes?" the older MacCowell answered.

The door opened and Meredoch's mother, Lynna, strode in with two of the Thane Denhard's honor guard. "Augustine, they're ready," Lynna announced, her eyes on her son.

"Very well, then." Augustine strode towards the door. Before reaching it, he turned back to Meredoch. "Lad, look after your mother and sister till I return."

"Yes, sir," Meredoch answered, eager and reluctant in one. A tear stung in his eye, but he willed it not to fall. When that failed, he turned his gaze to the wall by his bed.

Through shadows on his wall, he saw Sir Augustine nod and walk out with the two guards. Meredoch's mother stood halfway between the door and himself. Unable to help it, he swiped away the stubborn tear and looked at her. She wore a mothering look, as though she understood every bit of his anxiety about this meeting. But she couldn't know about the dreams, even if her expression held a shadow of his dread.

Meredoch's sister, Lydia, stirred at their mother's side, tugging on her dress.

Taking one of the young girl's hands, Lynna left the room. The remaining guards followed.

Meredoch sat on his bed, alone, staring at the huge grey stones forming the wall of his room. He gnawed at his lip, considering his windowless wall. Its thick stone kept him safe, wrapped securely in the arms of a mountain clothed in an imposing fortress. Safe, but blind.

Outside those walls, horse hooves pounded, and lines of warriors in gleaming armor marched. Trumpets announced the gallant rulers and all the regal airs demanded by the hour. Something else existed beyond the wall. Meredoch's gaze roved to a shelf on the far wall of the room. There his book of Ord history lay, fresh opened. If he hadn't been so eager for a childish game, he could have reminded his father what he read. What the Ecthels are in truth. "Traitors. Murderers. Monsters," he muttered and slung his pillow against the wall.

Not the kind that hid under a bed or scampered in the woods on full moon nights, but real monsters. The sort who killed for what they wanted and never found their want satisfied. Meredoch knew no force in the world could hurt him here. Save for his heart, which went with his father—out of the city, the fortress, and the mountain's hold, to reason with the unreasonable and tame a beast no Knight of Light or Ord had in over 300 years.

With a huff, Meredoch lay down on his bed, hoping to sleep through the horrid wait ahead. He rolled first onto his left side, then rolled onto his back, then his right. He huffed again and got up. From his shelf, he retrieved a weighty old tome and, back on his bed, cracked it open. *Eachdraidh, Histories.* The stories of the Orderer people, Ords for short, from the Ancient Era till present. Everything one could hope to know about the Ords' past was recorded here, including recent events, those chapters being freshly penned.

Huge, heavy, and thick with the scent of mold and memory, Meredoch had *liberated* it from the archives of the Ord's court historian.

Though the same instructors had tutored him as the Thane's son and the nobles of Ordumair, Meredoch wanted a fuller picture. The one from the source document itself. Looking over the scrawl of blockish characters, he had to focus. It was written in old Ord, something most Ords couldn't read now. He whispered aloud the first words with their rolling, consonant heavy sounds. Things soon flowed for him, and he began with the first entries, "Confluence of the Painted Warriors." A half-hour later, sleep claimed him, and once more, he found himself caught in a dream where his father stood at the head of the Ord armies, pushing their frontlines back. Augustine shouted, "Peace! There can be peace!" just before an Ecthel sword ran him through from behind.

"Meredoch, it's time to get up," a soothing voice called. His mother.

Meredoch mumbled, "Urfff," and ignored her. Three nights had passed since his father left, and every night the dreams of his father's demise tormented him.

His mother gave his uncovered arm a light shake. "Oh, my darling son, it's time to get up."

He didn't budge, sure he could outlast her.

"Oh, my sweet darling baby boy, do you need Mommy to help you up?"

Eyes open at a slit, he took in his mother's face. She smiled, but the tightness around her eyes let him know she wasn't as merry as she sounded. Something was off.

Meredoch heard a snicker from farther away. He stiffened and bolted upright. His best friend Duncoin, son of Denhard and heir apparent to the throne of Ordumair, stood in the doorway. By the looks of the huge grin on his slight dwarf face, Duncoin found Lynna's fawning hilarious.

Turning red, Meredoch grumbled. His mother's hands reached to grab him like a baby. He shooed them away. "Mother! Stop!"

Something akin to contentment shone in her eyes. Her small mouth quirked up in a smirk. "Oh, all right, darling little Merrydoch."

She stepped back and walked out of the room. Meredoch moaned after her, "Mother, please. I'm Meredoch, not a child." If Lynna heard, she gave no indication, not even looking back to receive Meredoch's fierce scowl.

For his part, thirteen-year-old Duncoin kept his amusement stowed away. Meredoch shot him the withering look. Heir apparent or not, Meredoch had a good head's height over Duncoin. A quick scrap would resolve the merrymaking at his expense. Pound for pound, in a fair fight, Duncoin would win. But Meredoch wasn't known for fighting fair, only for winning his share.

"Hale morning," Meredoch greeted and rolled out of bed.

"Hale, indeed," Duncoin replied, a ghost of his grin returning. "Forget about our sparring practice, did you?"

Meredoch's eyes widened. Both their fathers had set forth to neutral lands seeking the accord. No word had been sent back yet. Meredoch wondered how Duncoin could be so unconcerned about their fathers' fate. Then again, Meredoch was the one dreaming of death and sorrow. Foresight's specter sent a chill down Meredoch's back, and he shivered. From the way Duncoin's brow arched, his friend had noticed. He had to cover for it.

"How could I? You won't let me," Meredoch replied. Duncoin's expression told Meredoch he was not very successful. Quirking up his mouth in a smirk, he added, "I've never seen someone so eager to lose before."

To his relief, Duncoin took the baiting and spent the remainder of their trip through the fortress's wide, winding passageways boasting of how absolute his victory over Meredoch would be.

Duncoin was so absorbed in his jeers and bragging, he seemed oblivious to his friend's silence. Meredoch embraced the break from wearing a mask and thinking of the "right" things to say. He reminded himself the lack of word from the mediation wasn't unusual. Were it not for his dreams, he might have been able to relax.

"Hey, *Merrydoch,* is your head upon the summit?"

Glaring at Duncoin, Meredoch grumbled, "Doesn't it bother you, us stuck here while they're out there?"

"Who? Father and the soldiers?"

"Of course, them. They're about to face those beasts, and if we were older, we could be there, being of some use."

Duncoin stopped abruptly. "Instead of here, where we're training to join them when we are ready?"

Meredoch realized they were standing before the doors of the elite academy, where nobles among the Ords trained in war and command. On either door, the silver inlay of two combatants crossing blades loomed over them. Within, a private ring reserved for the Thane and any he deemed worthy centered the room. Duncoin had the freedom to use it, though this was the first time he stretched that rule and allowed Meredoch to spar with him.

The structure spanned two levels of the city. If it stood in an average town, it would have towered over a small castle. Broader than most Ordumair structures, the academy was built high into an outthrust of rock and deep within the mountain.

"Closer to the mountain's heart, the closer to glory," Meredoch recited. He drew in a breath and smiled at his friend.

"What are you talking about?"

"It's a proverb from the originator of the fortress and city, Thane Lowdrar, the Mad."

"Huh," Duncoin huffed. "And where did you learn that? I've never read anything about it."

Meredoch shrugged and focused his attention on the marble arcade that ran along either side of the doors. He gnawed his lip and hoped Duncoin didn't press about the source. His having the history book was something of a secret. At least his father had instructed him to keep it so. He blurted out, "See the blue tiling of lapis lazuli? Only the most venerated sites in Ordumair use them. The academy must be treasured, at least by those wealthy and important enough to see it."

Duncoin rolled his eyes. "Right, if you're done telling me all about my own people, perhaps we can go inside."

Despite his eagerness, Meredoch hesitated. "All the Thanes and Ord nobility since the fortress's construction trained for battle here. I'm not sure I'm allowed."

Duncoin slugged him in the arm. "Do no' worry. You are with me," the proud Ord reassured.

"I'm only worried about what they'll do when I totally disgrace you in our match." Meredoch jibed back, giving Duncoin a shove.

The doors swung open. A burly Ord with chestnut hair cut short and a beard down to his waist exited. The man's eyes narrowed at Meredoch, whose hands hung in the air from the playful shove. He quickly dropped them.

The Ord grunted. He turned toward Duncoin and gave a nod. "Your honor."

"Hale morning to you, Elder Ulster."

"Hale morning, indeed," he grumbled. "A haler morning, perhaps if we were both out on the lines facing our Ecthel foes instead of wringing our hands here while these Knights play parlay."

Meredoch swallowed and dropped his gaze. Ulster was only five or so inches taller than him but loomed over him like a giant.

"I'm sure my father only wishes the safety and hale of all," Meredoch replied, his gaze still down, and his voice not much more than a whisper.

Ulster bristled like a cat arching its back before hissing. His words were much harder than a hiss. "Your Order is strangling us. We are warriors, conquerors. Your father is as much an enemy to us as those blighted green fiends!"

"That's enough," Duncoin spoke up, his voice just as stony. "You forget my father is a Knight of Light himself, as are most of the elders on the Council. Prudence might be your best recourse right now."

Meredoch shot an appreciative glance at Duncoin. His friend's studies and grooming as his father's successor showed.

Ulster's sneer let Meredoch know he wasn't impressed. He turned to face Duncoin squarely and battered Meredoch with a broad shoulder as he did. Ulster's voice dropped an octave. "You presume much, young Duncoin. There are many lessons left before you can speak of such weighty matters with the Elders."

Duncoin swallowed, unable to hide his nervousness. Meredoch watched in silence. He locked his gaze on Ulster's dark eyes. The older man turned, again bumping Meredoch aside, and strode away.

Both boys let out shaky breaths. "Thanks," Meredoch said. He attempted to smile but failed. "My father wouldn't be pleased to know I've crossed the noble left as the reagent of Ordumair in the Thane's absence." Meredoch's father was Defender of the Northern Realm, the senior-most Knight in four countries—Albaron, Ordumair, Vogteremark, and Knorland. The territory spanned thousands of miles. Even so, the title had limits. "I know our being here isn't as welcome as in days past."

"You are the only non-Ords permitted to live in Ordumair," Duncoin affirmed. "But it's not you. He's trouble," he added, his voice low. "My father told me Ulster has been pushing the limits of the Council's powers. When I'm Thane, I know precisely where I'll stuff his lousy carcass."

Chuckling, Meredoch jabbed Duncoin. "Your father isn't the only Knight of Light. We aren't to speak so of others." Though secretly, Meredoch felt Elder Ulster might qualify as an exception.

Duncoin looked around and nodded. "You're right. We better get inside so I can crush you before lunch."

Meredoch frowned. There was something off about Duncoin just then, but he couldn't place it. Nor did he want to. "Okay. Everyone is entitled to fantasies."

Duncoin snorted, and the two laughed, and for the moment, put the encounter with Ulster behind them.

2

Another two days passed and still no word. Meredoch no longer hid his ill-ease about his father's delayed return. The tension wasn't just affecting him. He watched his mother fuss with his sister's hair and dress. *She never did that before.*

Sparring matches became a welcome distraction. Even if the wins officially fell to Duncoin. Meredoch claimed each was a draw. Each time Duncoin insisted on another match.

Duncoin looked quite smug today. Standing across the dueling circle from Meredoch, he rolled his gilded short sword over and over in his hand, making quick jabs for show. By now, the air was eviscerated, as Meredoch dithered over his weapon selection. Last time he had used a similar, if less ornate, short sword. He blamed the weapon for his poor performance yesterday, so he knew he couldn't get away with that this time. And he'd have to win today if he hoped to keep the sparring series going.

"Will you choose already? I 'aven't any desire to test the stone-tales."

Meredoch looked up from his search and scowled. "Stone-tales?"

"They're fables our parents told us when we're little to discourage us from being slothful." Duncoin heavily emphasized the latter. "If an Ord child stands idle too long, he risks being petrified and becoming part of the mountain."

Studying the weapons again, Meredoch mumbled to himself, "I'm sure many of your subjects are in the throes of grief that you're here with me instead of enriching their lives with your vast wit."

Rather than work the Ord up further, he answered with something less sarcastic. "How could I? You won't let me."

Meredoch's fingers drifted past one sword and lingered near the hilt. His fingertips tingled with nearness to the otherworldly weapon, the Spiritsword. Powerful blades inscribed with the very words of the High King, legendary for their sharpness, hardiness, and effectiveness in the hands of a Knight of Light. He'd heard that in a Knight's grasp, the sword would ignite and burn with fire from the High King.

"The perfect sword," Meredoch murmured.

Yet he was a mere "child," forbidden to use a Spiritsword. Their legendary power and potential were deemed as too much for the young. For him. At least in Ord society. Secretly, Meredoch's father taught him about them, even encouraged him to use the shortsword version stowed away in their home. It wasn't unlike this one.

"I will be as grey as Mount Fiorsruthain if you don't hurry up!"

Meredoch ground his teeth. He grabbed the Spiritsword and paused. *No flames?* His father promised in the hand of a Knight of Light, the High King's power would overtake the blade and set it afire.

He felt a tingle spread from his fingers to the nape of his neck. Suddenly, he felt a rush of warm air.

"Did you say something?" he called to Duncoin.

"You mean besides begging you to choose before I'm old enough to watch my grandchildren spar?"

Meredoch frowned. He thought he'd heard someone whisper to him. *Must be the air currents.* Stories circulated of mysterious voices in Ordumair. Vents carved into the mountain let in cooler outside air. Often people mistook the sound for voices, though some claimed they were the spirits of the Ords who died while slaving over the fortress's construction. He looked around. There had to be at least a few vents here.

"One problem with that gibe." Meredoch turned around. "You'd have to find a girl willing to take you before you can have children. Much less grandchildren."

"Only a problem if you're still crazy enough to think Caryn likes you more than me."

Grinding his teeth, Meredoch felt his cheeks redden. They both knew how he felt about Caryn. She was a head taller than all the other girls, and her red tresses glowed in the harvest sun. She was also the only Ord girl who didn't find Meredoch an anomaly. He felt a sudden pang of worry she might come in and see him lose this match.

Duncoin eyed Meredoch's choice of sword and smirked. "Feeling unduly confident, I see. You'll never succeed your father as Defender of the Realm with so little wisdom."

Shaking his head, Meredoch found his way back to the moment. "I believe you won't be smiling for long."

The dwarf didn't stop smiling. He dropped into a stance known as "The Bear," an aggressive Ord posture for combat said to have been first used by "The Bear" Thane Ordumair II in the Battle of Stalwart Timbers. That battle had been a decisive victory for the Ords over the Ecthels. All who fought it had since been nearly deified. Given Duncoin never adopted the style before, Meredoch decided his friend was the overconfident one.

Meredoch eased into a defensive posture common to Ords for single-weapon combat. "Well, let's see what you've got." He noticed Duncoin sliding a sleek, silver dagger out of an ornate sheath. The blade gleamed as the light caressed it.

"Where'd you get that?" Meredoch stalled, trying to figure a good counter to the added threat.

"A present from Elder Ulster." He twirled the dagger. "He came to me after I bested you yesterday. Made quite a long apology for the other day."

Like anything that man says is worth hearing.

Looking at his sword, Meredoch focused. Thinking about the odious Elder Ulster and the enchanting Caryn wouldn't win him this duel.

He stared at the Spiritsword and noticed that the blade's inscriptions, usually in the ancient language of the early Knight order, were written in Ord script. As with his book of histories, if he concentrated a bit, he could begin to make out the words.

"The High King is a strong tower," he read silently. The inscription read like poetry, but Meredoch carried it on his tongue like an invocation.

"Arrgh!"

His eyes flicked up to see Duncoin surging forward. Meredoch had unwittingly wandered into the circle designating the arena of combat. Gasping with shock and effort, he threw up a guard as Duncoin's heavy short sword hammered the Spiritsword.

The block took a lot of effort, and Meredoch found himself throwing up another and another, narrowly missing a sweeping blow that could have halved him. He leaped over a low swipe and crashed onto the floor. A quick roll spared him from being skewered as the silver dagger jabbed into the floor.

Someone is being tutored.

Seeing a wild overhead blow coming down, he met it just in time. Young Meredoch gritted his teeth and shoved against the Duncoin's pressure. His friend had taken an awful risk attacking when he was distracted, but it was in keeping with the fighting style. Mercy was not accorded to Ordumair The Bear, so tales told, and so mercy was not to be shown.

Slowly, the blades pushed closer and closer to Meredoch's chest. Struggle as he might, he could not break loose or overpower Duncoin. His friend's eyes were wild, seemingly unaware that the blades were now perilously close to cutting Meredoch.

It took all Meredoch's focus not to let them travel that half-inch more and slice him to ribbons. Had he been able to cry out, no one would hear him. They were alone. Did Duncoin mean to harm him?

I'm going to die!

Meredoch felt his muscles giving. Panic crept through his body.

This can't be happening. This can't be ... Help me, High King! Strong Tower, save me!

Suddenly everything slowed, and the room stretched until all was a blur. A blur more and more consumed by the brightest light Meredoch had ever seen. Then he saw him. Amidst a flash of fire and smoke sat a figure enthroned. Blinding brilliance swelled and overwhelmed Meredoch. Without a doubt, he was seeing the High King of All Realms.

He dropped to his knees, head bowed. "I'm sorry, sir," he blurted. "I didn't mean to ..."

Meredoch couldn't find words to describe his inadequacy before the Great King. He had seen great pomp and respect shown to the Thane and had been obliged to do the same at various festivities and feasts. He felt honored in the Thane's presence, but this was something wholly different. Meredoch's tongue ached in his mouth with the shame of thinking himself worthy of calling out to the High King.

Then a voice that burned and seared to the deepest core of his being echoed with the sound of breakers battering the rocky coastlands.

The Realms Rightful Ruler spoke to Meredoch, comforting him. A soothing sensation overtook much of the burn, but still, Meredoch didn't dare lift his eyes. "I'm sorry, Mighty King. I did not understand. I didn't know you before. I'm sorry for troubling you.

The voice of the King was both gentle as a summer breeze over the heather but stern as a sudden storm.

"I see. You cannot be called unless you were calling. Then please, my King, tell me what you want. Anything!"

For the moment, Meredoch's impending demise was a thousand leagues from his thoughts, and all that mattered was this. This encounter with majesty.

The boy listened as the Ancient One spoke. Meredoch's throat tightened, and tears rolled down his face. "You want me to pledge my loyalty to you? To become one of your Knights?"

There was a somberness to the reply that undercut the sudden joy and wonder Meredoch felt.

"Oh, I see. Even if that is what I may face, I make my pledge all the same. A hundred years or just this one, my life is yours in service."

The High King was suddenly close, close enough to reach out and touch Meredoch on one shoulder and then the other. Each burned as he never thought possible but did not hurt. The fire spread, tracing patterns familiar yet foreign down his extremities, across his whole body, centering over his chest. It pressed inside blazing paths along every sinew and bone till everything Meredoch felt he'd brought to this place was gone. Burned away.

He breathed in and out, expecting to see smoke pour from his mouth and taste its acrid tails, but the breath that went out and the air that came in was sweeter than he could describe.

He heard one last command: Rise, Sir Meredoch MacCowell.

Then, the light flared even brighter, and Meredoch could see nothing, but also everything. The world resolved back to the one he had left, back to the contest of wills. Duncoin's feral intensity still etched into his expression. The pressure of the blades against each other still taxing Meredoch's muscles. But he no longer felt weakness in his limbs. Only fire. A fire that traveled down to the Spiritsword or perhaps up from it.

The sensation built and built until Meredoch cried out and slung his opponent off of him.

Meredoch's chest heaved, drawing in deep breaths. Mesmerized, he watched flames dance along his blade, its inscriptions glowing with fiery glee. He looked past the blade to Duncoin. The exultant smile he wore had faded.

Duncoin stared at him, his mouth slack.

"Duncoin, I had the vision!" Meredoch said too quickly and sucked in a much-needed breath. Slower, he had to slow himself. "I had the vision of the Great King. I joined the Order. Have you always been able to see these flames? And ... and ..." Meredoch faltered for words. There was more. So much more. It wasn't just the blade that was different. Everything was sharper, redefined as though he had never truly seen it properly before. All the familiar contours and surfaces of the only home, the only world he had ever known, greeted him as for the first time.

His chest shuddered as he drew in another awed breath.

At last, his eyes roamed back to Duncoin. The Ord still lay on the ground, his dumbfounded expression replaced by something more guarded. As though Meredoch were some kind of lunatic. Or at least a beast he was unfamiliar with and therefore could neither welcome nor ward off effectively.

"Duncoin?" Meredoch reached out a hand and stepped toward his friend.

Duncoin took the offered hand and struggled up. He let the sword he'd wielded clatter to the floor, and Meredoch noticed the dagger from Elder Ulster had been shattered and lay smoldering a few feet away.

Before either youth spoke again, the doors to the training structure swung open and smashed against the stone walls. A trio of soldiers burst into the room. They spread out as if searching for something. One spotted Duncoin and called out, "We've found him. He's in here!"

Two more guards rushed in, and Elder Ulster followed at their heels.

The old Ord's sharp eyes scanned the room and fell first on Duncoin, then Meredoch, still holding the Spiritsword. They narrowed fractionally. "Disarm him and take him to the dungeon. Bring the Thane."

Before another heartbeat passed, Ulster whirled around and exited.

Meredoch and Duncoin stared wide-eyed at each other as the first three soldiers flanked Duncoin and escorted him out with gentle firmness. Meredoch's last sight of his friend was Duncoin straining to look back and uttering a question that got lost to Meredoch as the other pair of soldiers swung their halberds round and shouted, "Drop your sword. NOW!"

Meredoch couldn't comprehend the order. This was a training room, and the soldiers were in a combat stance reserved for dangerous enemies.

What is going on?

"I said NOW!"

A faint whisper of a now-familiar voice gusted past Meredoch's ear, telling him to comply. He put the sword down.

The two Ords rushed forward and grabbed him roughly by his arms, forcing each behind his back before closing heavy iron shackles around his wrists. They barely fit, being made for adult Ord wrists, but it wouldn't have mattered if they were the tightest restraints in the world. The chill of the iron on his skin felt like a viper's strike. The numbness of the blow spread throughout him. Try as he might to be tough, a single tear slid free and ran down his cheek as he was towed out of the room.

3

Meredoch stretched, awareness of his surroundings and memory of the events from the preceding night crashed down on him. Their weight crushed the air from him into something between a sigh and a moan. He was alone, in the darkest, most odious place he could imagine. Worse, he understood all too clearly he might never see his family again.

Reaching out to his right, he found one of his cell walls. Meredoch ran his hands over the stone, feeling its jagged contours. The rock was slick with moisture dripping from somewhere. He quickly rubbed it off against his pants. This place was far different from the smooth cut room he had grown up in. He used to rub his bedroom wall and think about the ten thousand Ords who gave their lives in the construction of the fortress.

From the painstaking attention to detail and quality elsewhere, Meredoch believed they died from exhaustion and with great suffering. A notion his father had never tried to dispel. Now a sickening worry that perhaps he had been thrown in some unfinished portion of the fortress enveloped him. Left with the bodies of workers who died trying to complete an impossible task.

He could only guess, but Meredoch felt days had passed since he had been brought down into the dungeon. No one answered his questions. Barely any food or water had been brought to him. A haze hovered around every meal he received. Thinking on it made his head throb.

Even a few words of accusation would have been a welcome break from the breathy wheeze of musty air over the rocks. A distant water drip added to Meredoch's madness. Some time ago, he stopped asking why. It was futile. He had even stopped rehashing the events of recent days. Instead, he thought about that moment before his arrest. His vision. It was more than he could fully grasp. It helped to remember that moment and the fire of the High King in this chilly, awful place.

Meredoch adjusted himself to a more comfortable position on the jagged rocks. A loud clang and dull banging sound echoed throughout the large cavern. Unsure what it implied, Meredoch bolted upright. His eyes strained with hopefulness. He squinted against a growing point of light in the room's dark matte expanse. The light bounced and swayed erratically before resolving itself into the form of a middle-aged Ord with a bushy brown beard and deep blue eyes.

"Elder Orwald, sir!" Meredoch's voice cracked from thirst and lack of use.

By the light of the torch Elder Orwald carried, Meredoch could make out a scowl passing over his features.

"Lad, no need to put a good face on it. I'm sure you've seen better days than this."

"I suppose I have, sir."

"I apologize for that. We Ords weren't known as such poor hosts in days past."

An uncomfortable silence fell on them.

Uncomfortable, because Elder Orwald was silent and the lit contours of his face twisted as if he were gnawing his lip. Meredoch wasn't sure what to make of this visit. His father taught him to be respectful of the Elder, who was doubtless the most gracious friend to the Order. Seeing him out of sorts puzzled Merdoch. He felt shaky and reached toward Orwald for support. His hands bounced off the slick iron cell bars. Meredoch fought to catch himself and stumbled.

"Lad, are you all right?" Orwald tried to steady Meredoch through the bars, but the spacing was too narrow.

"Where is my father?" Meredoch pleaded.

Elder Orwald straightened. He grew very still and stiff. "Your father and mother and sister are being held in other cells. Soon to be released, if I have anything to say about it."

"Father is here? Is he well? Is there peace?"

In the flickering light, Orwald's face appeared as stony as the mountain. The Elder offered no response. None was needed. Had all gone well none of this, whatever "this" was, would have happened.

Meredoch changed tactics, his voice imploring, "What happened? Why were we locked up in Ordumair's dungeons like criminals?"

"Strictly speaking," Orwald deflected, "You aren't in Ordumair. This is unfinished jailing at the valley entry's outpost."

"But how did I get here?" Confused, Meredoch mumbled, searching about as if his surroundings could somehow give him the answers.

Orwald grumbled and seemed to break free of some

invisible bonds. "Bother it all. You deserve the truth. You've been ... drugged. For a few weeks now."

"Weeks!? I was poisoned?"

Nodding, Orwald continued in a somber voice. "Belladonna. Small doses. The guards slipped it into your meals every time you woke since you were first taken into custody."

Meredoch tried to remember, but everything after being taken from the training room was a blur. Keeping just out of reach like a fish in murky water. "They were trying to kill me?"

"At first, yes," Orwald admitted. "They aren't sure why it failed the first times they tried it, but I suspect it is because the High King's power is protecting you."

"Duncoin told you about me having a vision and the Spiritsword burning and ..." Meredoch realized rambling like this wasn't helpful. In more composed tones, he asked, "So, he told you? Does that mean he knows I'm here?"

For a few seconds, Orwald did not answer, seeming to regard Meredoch warily. His eventual answer was short. "No."

Nodding, Meredoch remembered one thing as though it had been chained to a weight and freed to rise to the surface. "Did Duncoin become Thane?"

Bristling, Orwald asked in a low voice, "How do you know of that?"

"Elder Ulster told the soldiers to 'Bring the Thane' when I was arrested." Meredoch paused. That word 'arrested' felt impossible to fit with himself. He was just a kid. What had he done besides using a Spiritsword? Surely that was frowned upon, not worthy of a dungeon.

"When they grabbed Duncoin right after me, I just put it together. Sorry, Thane Duncoin, may he long reign." Taught to say that last bit when mentioning a Thane felt even more bizarre when he spoke the words. Duncoin was his friend, not some dignitary beyond approach. However, he must be now if Meredoch was here and the target of murder. Tears rolled down Meredoch's cheeks, no matter his efforts to stop them. Soon he was sobbing and dropped to the ground, his back to the cell bars, head between his knees. "Why is this happening?"

"I'm sorry lad. There are circumstances you wouldn't understand, and I will not burden you with it. But you must know a few things.

"One, my brother, Thane Denhard, was mortally wounded when the peace talks became violent. He was brought to Ordumair and died an hour ago. I've been acting regent, but that will end shortly.

"Two, your family cannot stay. A horrible siege took place after the attack on my brother. Your father counseled us to not abandon peace. The Ecthels rebuffed us and cut us off. Many people are suffering. Food is scarce. Your family is no longer welcome. Very soon, they will come to torture and then kill you all. I am here to help you escape that fate.

"Third, hold out your hand, because I am entrusting you with something you must never show anyone."

Meredoch looked up and saw Orwald holding something in pincer grasp between the bars. It glinted in the light of his torch —a ring. Meredoch raised a shaking hand, and the Elder dropped the ring into Meredoch's palm.

"What is this?" Meredoch managed between suppressed sniffles.

"The Signet of Thanes. My brother gave it to me when he arrived. We both believe it is too dangerous to keep here any longer."

"But it's just a ring," Meredoch wiped his eyes and nose with a sleeve.

"Nay. It is a symbol. Our people are very proud. Very stubborn, some might say. Our traditions define us. Whoever possesses this ring is obeyed by many as Thane, no matter bloodline and succession rules. You cannot understand it now, but what you told me confirms the ring can only mean danger to us. You must keep it. Can you do that, Sir Meredoch?"

At the use of his knightly title, Meredoch raised to his feet. He felt a little woozy. "I think so, sir."

"Do not just *think* it, *do* it, lad. Tell no one of the signet. Not even your family. Promise me this."

"I promise," he replied, though still unsteady.

Pursing his lips, Orwald nodded. "Then this shall be your first quest as a Knight of Light. May it not be the last."

Meredoch's eyes widened, and he knew a smile, weak but genuine, found its way to his face.

Elder Orwald busied himself about some keys and unlocked a door to the cell Meredoch had not even seen.

When the door creaked open, Orwald waved a brawny arm for Meredoch to come. "Hurry, we must get to your parents and get you all out of Ord lands before daybreak."

Realization struck Meredoch as he followed Orwald at a hurried pace. "You aren't supposed to be doing this, are you?"

"No."

"How will we get past this prison's guards?" Before Orwald could even reply, Meredoch exclaimed, "Oh, the secret tunnels!"

"You know of them?" Orwald asked, surprised.

"I know them," Meredoch replied, a smirk on his face.

Elder Orwald sighed. "My nephew is indiscreet in sharing my people's most guarded secrets. May the High King grant that he learn prudence swiftly."

"In his defense, aren't you about to do the same?"

Pausing to look back at Meredoch, the old Ord's face was taut. As if he fought hard not to smirk. "Follow me."

PART II

———

FRESH BLOOD

4

Eight years later
Year 1565 of the Middle Era

A foul odor permeated the air in Wyvern's Breath Tavern, a smell now familiar to Meredoch. But acclimating himself to the noise and "colorful" characters who frequented the Wyvern's Breath Tavern was more difficult. Seeking refuge from the rain, Meredoch edged around two fat old drunks, passed out near the entrance, tankards still in hand.

Shaking chilly droplets from his cloak onto them, he rolled his eyes when they failed to stir. He ran his fingers through his short, cropped hair and sighed. Things were rowdier than usual tonight.

He shouldered through another group near the entrance, these throwing knives at a target board. Not more than ten steps further into the building, he felt a tug on his arm. A hefty blonde woman stood beside him.

"Hey there, handsome." She puffed out her deep maroon lips. "Can I get you anything?"

Meredoch smiled and extricated his arm. "No, Helene. I'm here to collect him again."

"Oh, too bad," she replied as she always did before giving him a slight bump with her hip. She moved on to assist her establishment's other patrons.

No matter how often he came, this wasn't easy. Meredoch took in a few steadying breaths and kept moving, ignoring the stares. Gossip about him and the flirty owner would sprout like weeds around him and die with the speakers' memories of this night.

Something of more immediate importance sat a few dozen feet away. Wild coarse hair covered the old man's head lying on the bar. He was a crafty man, so awake or not, Meredoch knew his task wouldn't be easy.

A flaxen-haired maiden rested a hand on the old man's back. As Meredoch neared, she looked up. Her brown eyes filled with apology. He held up a hand. This wasn't Lydia's doing.

She nodded and rose carefully, trying not to alert the man. The young woman smoothed her saffron dress's billows and gave Meredoch a little half curtsy. As she passed by, she gave him a light kiss on the cheek and whispered, "Go easy on him."

Meredoch watched her until she left the building. Her dress was the most modest outfit in the drinking hole, but Lydia was young and beautiful by any standard. Moreover, Meredoch was acutely aware of her dress's cost. He had given it to her, after all.

He returned his attention to his quarry. The old man sat upright and stared him down with hard, hazel eyes. Meredoch's eyes.

"Father, I've come to collect you." Even as he said it,

Meredoch swallowed back his nerves. Twenty years old, a man in his own right, yet he could barely face this shell of a man—a man who scarce resembled the father of his youth.

"Why are you here, boy?" Meredoch's father grumbled, his once impressive frame now ravaged by almost a decade of drink and despair. "Did your sister put you up to this? Where did she scurry to anyway? My coins are all—"

He fumbled in his dirty robe's pockets and produced a few bits, which he cackled triumphantly at and slammed down on the counter. "Another round, Lumond."

The keeper looked warily at Meredoch for approval and seeing the scowl Meredoch gave him, backed up a few paces. "Sorry, Despero. You will have to find your ale elsewhere."

The man had discreetly pocketed the money all the same. Despero, once known as Augustine MacCowell, didn't notice. His angry, unfocused eyes bore down on Meredoch. "You cannot give me a day's peace, can you? One day to forget my troubles and ..."

In recent years, Augustine had dubbed himself Despero. It suited him. Despero attempted to stand and loom over Meredoch as he had years ago. He stumbled.

Swooping to steady the man he'd outgrown, Meredoch restrained him in one move.

Seconds later, his father flailed wildly, throwing elbows, twisting and smashing limbs against Meredoch with surprising force for his withered state.

"Let me go! Let me go, you—you—"

Meredoch hoisted his father slightly off the ground, cutting off the man's ability to speak, and dead-lifted him out of the room.

The elder MacCowell retched.

Meredoch maneuvered to avoid spraying other patrons and himself with the putrid matter. They reached the door. Helene held it open, a rueful look on her face. "Take care of him, darling," she said.

"Darling? He's nothing but a churl? The son of a—"

Meredoch didn't wait to hear whatever foul thing was about to come out of his father's mouth. Slinging him around to land outside in the rain, Meredoch grabbed the tavern door and slammed it shut.

5

"I told you to be gentle." Lydia examined the handful of contusions on their father, results of Meredoch's scuffle during the journey home. "He doesn't mean what he says, you know."

Meredoch didn't answer. She enabled their father's destructive self-loathing with her tenderness. He enabled her destructive naiveté with his.

"Meredoch, what do you have to say for yourself?"

He rolled his eyes. Ever since their mother died suddenly, his sister assumed the family's matriarchal role. And though he fell in line most of the time, on this Meredoch could not yield. "He was going to curse me by degrading her. I tolerate a lot from him, but not that. Never that."

His sister looked down. Tears welled in her eyes. She was still his little sister, whatever bravery and maturity she put on. At sixteen, Lydia ran their father's house. A house Meredoch had fled at the first chance. Albeit his flight was to embrace a noble work, his Quest, he was sure.

In his myriad studies and devotion to the High King,

Meredoch was poised to become the new Defender of the Realm. Succeeding a position left vacant since his father abandoned it the year his mother died. "Too much failure, too much heartache," said the elders of their Order.

Out of respect for Augustine's past honor, they did not strip him of the title or seek the High King's guidance bestowing it to another. Until now. Now that Augustine MacCowell's son had shown himself a worthy heir to the family name and the work his father forsook.

Meredoch sighed and collapsed next to his sister, wrapping his arms around her. "Don't cry, Lydie," he soothed. "All will be well. You're right. It will all pass."

He did not consider it a lie so much as a wish. It seemed effective, as Lydia soon brushed aside her tears with soft-skinned knuckles. Out of nowhere, she laughed. "I'm sixteen, and you still call me 'Lydie.' There are girls my age readying to marry."

Meredoch grunted. "And there are girls your age who don't have me as their big brother."

He pulled her into a tight hug and mussed her straight golden locks till they were a frizzy, poofed mess.

She laughed the whole while but put her hands on her hips as if indignant. "And *this* is why I'll never find a suitor."

He forced the sadness from creeping into his expression. More like she'd never find one with their father dragging her down. This was how things were of late. Always dancing around melancholy and smiling even when in jester's garb, it smacked them in the face.

"Bah, didn't I see William skulking around outside the other day, mustering the courage to offer you some flowers?"

"William, ah, bleh, no. He was probably shuffling his feet as he worked himself up to wooing Neeony.

"Though if Robere were to show up, you will have to find

someone else to manage things here. Just thinking about those dreamy eyes and kind mouth and ..."

"Right, right. Consider the subject officially beyond my thoughts. Indefinitely." They both laughed. Lydia pulled herself up. "And what about you, old man MacCowell? Where is your bride? Don't tell me you've missed the way Corinna stares at you every time you come home. Gwynlyn has it worse for you, I hear."

"Oh, yes, Gwynlyn. Those sky-blue eyes, rosy cheeks, cherry lips ..." he thought she would interrupt him as he had her, but she moved from jest into an attempt at mothering him.

Meredoch rolled his eyes. "Sister, clearly, you're forgetting that between filling my oaths for the Order and visits home, the only women I've spent any time with are you and Helene."

Lydia wrinkled her nose, "Please don't pursue Helene's hand. Her husband Lumond might object."

They laughed together until their father stirred beside them, crying out in his sleep, "No! Denhard! Get him out. Not my fault. Not my fault—"

Meredoch closed his eyes and turned away. These night terrors were too familiar a sound. Behind him, Lydia rushed to their father's side and soothed. "Papa, papa, you're safe. Everything is all right. We know it's not your fault."

The sound of her gentle voice scoured Meredoch like a raptor's claws digging into its prey.

Once Despero had quieted, she returned. "I think he'll be all right now."

"None of us will ever be all right," Meredoch challenged. His hand automatically fumbled into the pouch he had on his belt, where he kept it. The relic from Ordumair. Its smooth contours were familiar, as was the stylized tree and dual fountains engraved on it.

"Don't say that," she pleaded, her voice just a whisper. "Mother wouldn't want you to give up."

His throat tightened, and his hand mimicked, closing around the signet. "There are a lot of things mother wouldn't have wanted." Meredoch's eyes fell hard on his sister, and he immediately regretted it. On the verge of tears, Lydia didn't look as motherly as she tried to sound. She looked like a child. A little girl, playing house who needed someone to tell her everything was fine. He should have assured her of just that, but instead, he felt a swell of anger rippling through him.

The fury emanated from his palm, which pressed hard on the ring. That same absurd ring he'd guarded all these years for the very people who had ruined his family. In his hand, the small signet suddenly felt heavier. As if enchanted to drag down him and all who had unjustly carried it from Ord lands. A protest bristled in his mind at the ring's phantom accusation.

"Arrgh!" He slung the ring across the room. It clanged off a wall and out of sight.

Though he wanted its burdensome weight off him, Meredoch only felt it all the more. He collapsed onto a nearby stool and put his head in his hands. No tears came. They couldn't. Those were spent long ago when he was just a child. All he felt now was the gall of his fading fury.

"Merry?" Lydia inquired.

The hesitance in her voice snapped him back to the present. He looked at her, and on top of all the other pain she carried was a fresh welt from fear. "I'm just like him," Meredoch muttered. "I'm a beast just like him."

"Like father?"

Even if he weren't choked beyond words, her question didn't need an answer. She knew. "You're not a beast. Neither of you is."

"You can't see what you don't want to," he insisted, but

somehow her assurance was enough to pull his head out of his hands. To help him get his head above the seas of his shame again.

Sighing, Lydia placed a hand on Meredoch's back, gentle as a leaf landing on the water. "Maybe we should go for a walk? The cherry blossoms are in bloom." When Meredoch remained locked in his stony reticence, she added, "You know how I love them."

Pursing his lips, Meredoch nodded. "I do. Mother loved them as well."

He stared into the imploring eyes of his sister and stood. Offering her an arm, he escorted her out. As he pulled the door shut, he thought he saw his father stir and sit upright. Meredoch considered going back in to ask him along but instead pulled the door shut all the tighter.

Six warriors, all armed and closing in with remarkable uniformity, encircled Meredoch. He held his blade level, parallel to the ground, the flames crackling around the blade's length.

Two men had spears, one an axe, the others, swords with barbs along the curvature. All capable warriors and all would be upon him in seconds. Pivoting slowly, Meredoch spied the formation's weak point. Leaping, he barreled forward and smashed shoulder first into the axe-wielder.

Caught off-guard by the bold and dangerous gambit, the axe dropped from the wielder's hand as he tumbled backward to the ground.

Spinning around, Meredoch deflected a jab from a spear. Bringing his Spiritsword crackling around, he smashed it overhead into the spear shaft, severing it in two. Before the attacker could recover, Meredoch grabbed the man and slung him around and down to the ground, blocking a swordsman from sneaking up on his flank.

Meredoch ducked past the next swordsman and swung his

sword, battering aside the tip of the remaining spearman's weapon. Faster than a blink, he brought the burning blade in his hands back up in an arc that cut the spear in half, forcing its user to back up and trip over the first spearman.

The swordsman behind him maneuvered around his bested compatriot and charged with a furious cry. Meredoch sidestepped, blocked the attack, and spun around behind the man, knocking him on his face with the pommel of the Spiritsword.

One foe remained. Facing the final sword-bearer, Meredoch straightened and walked slowly forward. A boy, around twelve years old, stood at an uneasy guard before him. "Are my King's enemies using children now?"

From several yards away, three figures approached. The eldest, a stiff old man with deep blue eyes and dark skin like worn leather, strode forward. Omelek. He had spent his entire life as a Knight Errant in the North, traveling from region to region, instructing new generations of Knights to bolster the Order. Unlike Order chapters in far eastern realms, there was no concept of squire ascending to knighthood for Meredoch. Rather, mentorship was emphasized with all Knights viewed as equals. At least in principle. For more than a year, Omelek had been Meredoch's mentor.

Standing a little straighter, Meredoch looked on the elder Knight with expectant eyes. Omelek radiated warmth in all his interactions. Meredoch often explained to others, "He makes you feel like his friend on first meeting." So different from Meredoch, who one elder had called, "A very heroic statue."

Omelek didn't tip his hand about his thoughts, though everyone in the room fell silent, waiting for them. No one in the Vogteremark could better determine Meredoch's fitness. If chosen to assume his father's former mantle, Meredoch would be the youngest Defender of the Realm in nearly four centuries.

Clearing his throat, Omelek spoke in his surprisingly high voice, "What you will face may surprise you. When you shine light in the dark, be ready when that which stalks in it bears fangs."

Nodding, Meredoch stared at the ground, his jaw clenched.

Omelek must have noticed. "You disagree, young MacCowell?"

Meredoch swallowed. He considered lying but thought better of it. "I'm ready for any opponent, but even fiends would not fight using children."

Stepping forward, Omelek gazed into Meredoch's eyes. "You did not hear me. Your fight is not with men, but monsters. They will not make this fight fair or easy or obvious. You will see things that are not what they are in truth. If you are not careful, the deceit will claim you."

The old man withdrew, seized by a hacking cough fit. They were becoming more frequent in recent weeks. Regaining his composure, Omelek looked Meredoch up and down once more. Lips pursed, he murmured, "I have seen enough. You're quite imposing, young MacCowell. But you lack something. Before you can be entrusted the blessing and burden of becoming Defender of the Realm, you must complete one task: Make peace with Ordumair."

Meredoch gaped. The elder may well have asked him to lift the sun higher or blot out the moon. His eyes darted to the other elders for support and found them looking just as shocked.

"Make peace with them? Has no one told you what happened there when I was a boy?" He knew the elder was well aware. How could the man dare ask him to go back? They might well kill him. No outsider had entered Ordumair since his family's exile.

Worse, part of him spoiled for the fight. His outburst of slinging the signet ring just days before was still a tender wound, fresh in his mind. Seeing the Ords, whose actions made the worst of him, couldn't be good for anyone.

"I have heard much. But we both know you have the one thing that will bring the peace you both need."

Peace? He considered the word, imagined its sensation, a lightness so sweetly tempting. He must have been longing for it, unawares, for some years. But what did he have?

Silently, Meredoch mouthed, "The Signet of Thanes!"

Sir Omelek's eyes narrowed, but he said nothing. Then, he turned and walked away.

"Sir, is there no other way?" Meredoch called after him.

Pausing, Omelek replied without looking back, "No. You must face this darkness before you can bear the Northlands' light." Then he strode away again.

Meredoch considered following but decided against it. The Knight Errant had seemed sure. If Meredoch was going to redeem his family name and find peace, first, he had to get home right away.

ARRIVING at his father's house, Meredoch barely waited on Lydia to open the door before he crashed through. Remembering his outburst vividly, he headed directly for where he'd thrown the signet more than a week earlier. He had a dim awareness that his sister had leaped back in surprise and clasped her hand over her chest.

He said nothing and slammed his fist against the wall over where he believed the ring should lay.

Lydia spoke. "Merry, what are you doing? Is everything—"

"Where is the ring?"

"Ring? You mean—"

"The one I threw. The Signet of Thanes. Where is it?"

"I'm not sure. After our walk, I forgot about everything. I was awfully busy and—"

"We have to find it." Meredoch ran shaky hands through his hair. "We have to find it now."

"Stop and tell me what's going on."

"Sir Omelek won't grant me the title until I make peace with the Ords, and that ring is the key. We have to find it." He laced his fingers behind his head and glanced around. Something felt off about the room. Some detail of the incident was missing from the present scene.

Before Lydia could speak, he asked, "Where's Father?"

7

─────

Dark was fast approaching. After four days spent in the search for their father, exhaustion encased Meredoch. Sometime around noon of the second day, one of Despero's drinking "friends" revealed he left for a small village south of Estonbury, Bracken.

A light rain, cool and persistent, pelted Meredoch as he led Corona, Lydia's horse, through the copse surrounding the town. The town's namesake vegetation grew scraggly and gnarled, its bark darker in the storm. Atop the horse, his sister fidgeted quietly with the saddle cantle.

Bracken wasn't the sort of place he would normally take his sister. Then again, it didn't seem like the ideal place to sell the Signet of Thanes unless Despero already found a buyer. How could he have located one so quickly, though? And who could want it? Only Ords cared for it, though it was partly cast from gold and could turn a tidy profit to a petty thief. The term "petty thief" and how it now fit his father jostled around in Meredoch's mind as they approached the village.

The town was small, much smaller than any town

47

Meredoch had seen. Living in Estonbury and Sorgby after Ordumair, Meredoch couldn't say how it compared to other villages, but with only ten buildings, it was far from impressive. Only one structure stood over a story tall, an inn and tavern by the look of it.

Gentle lantern lights cast their faint auras onto the ashen evening, creating a strange homely sense. A faint hint of cedar mingled amidst the damp wood smells. Meredoch wondered if the little swirls of smoke drifting lackadaisically from the chimneys carried the scent.

By the time he tethered the horse to a hitch and helped Lydia down, a rotund man with wispy blonde hair strode out. His rosy cheeks were pulled up in a beaming smile.

"Greetings! Welcome to Bracken, young travelers."

"Greetings," Meredoch replied, a bit unsure.

The other man studied him for a bit. "I hope you don't mind me saying so, friend. But you remind me of Cinaed."

Meredoch flicked a glance at his sister. She seemed distant. Straightening, he replied, "The hero from legends of Tislatna? High praise."

"Actually, my nephew, of much humbler exploit," the man amended. "You bear a striking resemblance."

"Oh." The awkwardness of moments before fell over him.

The man must have picked up on it. "Is there something I can help you with?"

Meredoch looked at Lydia again. She gave a slight shrug. Neither was accustomed to such congeniality from strangers. "We're looking for our father. Augustine MacCowell."

The man rubbed his chin thoughtfully. "The name isn't one I've heard of late. Are you sure he was passing through these parts?"

"Positive," Meredoch replied. "He should have arrived by last night at the latest."

"The only recent arrival was a fairly disheveled man. Went by the name Despero I be—"

"That's him!"

"Ah, well, you missed him by a couple of hours. He went on foot southwest toward Pin Creek."

"Thank you." Meredoch whirled to face his sister. "Stay here. I'll get him."

Lydia scowled. "Don't hurt him. He made a mistake." She reached over and placed a gentle hand on Meredoch's arm. "We all do."

"I promise to bring him back unharmed." Meredoch mounted the horse. To the man, he instructed, "Kind sir, please see to it my sister is given a fine room at the inn, and no one mistreats her. I'll pay handsomely on my return."

A stretch perhaps, but the man simply doffed a light green cap he wore. "The name is Edward, by the way. To Lydia, he added, "Edward Goodby at your service." He directed her toward the inn. Before Meredoch was out of earshot, he heard his sister ask, "How is it you know all the travelers here?"

"Bracken strives to see everyone finds warmth and welcome when away from home ..." The rest was lost as Meredoch spurred the horse on. Even with his father on foot, a few hours could put him at his meeting place by now. Tracking him wouldn't be easy, particularly given how swiftly the night closed in.

8

To Meredoch's relief, gentle plains rolled across the vast majority of the land to the south and west. He took in the tall grasses swaying under a steady breeze, like a green sea around him, stretching for miles in each direction. It would have been pleasant, but all Meredoch could feel or think about was the heat of his anger. Keeping his promise to his sister would not be easy. Despero was not his father. Not the one he had loved and respected and idolized as a child.

That man was dead so far as Meredoch could tell. All that remained was a black mark on his father's name. His family's name. On the High King's name. Despero may care nothing for any of those, but Meredoch was determined to be nothing like him.

Just as night fell, Meredoch spotted a figure, stumbling along in the high grasses toward a small copse that covered the highest knoll in the landscape. *Despero.* Dropping from his horse and letting it munch on the grass, Meredoch walked the remaining distance to keep from alerting his father too soon.

Darkness enveloped his father's meandering path through the wood. Meredoch followed to a small clearing that looked manmade rather than a natural feature. To one side, under the branches of some trees stood a large, mossy rock.

Despero stood at the glade's center, fidgeting. Meredoch imagined he must have reached his meeting point. *If I'm patient, I can apprehend Despero and his buyer. Anyone who would buy such a thing from that treacherous sot can't be too far from a thieves' den.*

Climbing into the concealing boughs of a large cedar, Meredoch watched and waited with Despero. When it grew so dark he could scarcely see, things took a turn for the strange. Cooler winds cut across the clearing and set the trees quivering as if in fright. A sound, like stone cracking, echoed from within the enclosure. A groan, horrid as that of the dying, followed it, along with a stench like putrefying vegetation.

The rock moved. Didn't just move but stood erect. Tall, taller than Despero, taller than any man Meredoch had ever met. The rock grunted. Hot jets of steam emitted from each nostril, visible for the sudden coolness enwrapping the glade. The thing spoke. "So, my employers told the truth. Fallen son of light, did you bring your part of the bargain?"

From behind the spindly cedar, Meredoch watched the grand spectacle. Sir Augustine MacCowell, once Defender of the Realm, held out his hand to the most loathsome creature Meredoch had ever seen. His father's offering betrayed everything he'd sworn to defend.

The creature's great thick fingers curled around the ring. A laugh rumbled from deep within, cruel and keening. "My, my, this is rich. Those Ords will pay a fanciful price for this."

Interrupting the fit of chortling, Meredoch heard Despero speak. "No. The deal was you would sell it to the Ecthels. Either follow our agreement or hand it back over."

The chortling stopped, replaced by a fit of raucous laughter. The laughter must have touched a nerve, because before Meredoch could fully process it, Despero had drawn a short sword and moved against the hulking beast.

With one swipe of a thick arm, the beast sent Despero sailing across the glade. He tumbled in a heap, like one of Lydia's childhood rag dolls. The creature stopped laughing. It stalked over to Despero. Its lope was so slow, Despero had time to stand. He took another swipe, and from the sound of the clatter and dark dots that dropped in the distance, the sword broke on the thing's rocky hide. This time, the creature hoisted Despero into the air and tossed him into a tree with a sickening crunch.

Meredoch tasted bile in his throat. His heart raced for action, but his body remained paralyzed. The creature spat on the prone Despero. "Tomorrow, I'll be giving this to an Ord elder who has big plans for it. Big plans worth paying a tiny fortune. You should've kept your mouth shut, and maybe I would've shared."

As an afterthought, the creature chuckled again, sick and gleefully. "Probably not." It stalked off and was gone, deep into the woods beyond before Meredoch broke from his stunned stupor. *Had he just watched a monster meet with his father?* No, worse, *murder* his father?

Climbing down, he dashed over to Despero. Meredoch drew his Spiritsword, the fire caught along the blade immediately and created a halo of light around himself and his fallen father. Bending over Despero, unsure what to do, Meredoch heard the faint sounds of labored breathing.

Tears slipped down his cheeks before he could rein them in. He wiped them away with his armored forearm. Meredoch's breath caught as he also saw the bleeding and breakages evident from the attack. Whatever attacked his father was incredibly strong and unbearably cruel.

"Meredoch ..." Despero's voice was like the voice of the grave, raspy and low.

"Yes, father?" Meredoch could scarcely look him in the eyes.

A shaking hand grabbed at Meredoch's forearm and held onto the smooth armor there, trembling. "The boggart ... mustn't let the boggart ..." Then the old man went limp, and for an instant, Meredoch despaired that he had died. But again, the weak sounds of breathing told him otherwise.

Unsure what else to do, Meredoch hoisted his father into his arms and carried him back to his horse. A horrid storm of emotions swirled within him, prompted by two things. One, his father's body felt much too limp, too frail in his arms, not the symbol of strength he was born to be. Second, his father's last words might not be of love or repentance or comfort or blessing. Instead, the last thing his father would likely utter were mad ravings about a creature that shouldn't exist.

9

———

Edward sat at the table across from Meredoch and Lydia. From the heaviness of his expression, he did not have good news. The man said nothing.

"How is he?" Lydia asked, unable to resist hope's pull.

"Not good, I'm afraid. There is much more injury to your father's body than my limited skills can mend. When men suffered lesser injuries than this on the battlefield, we just made them comfortable."

Lydia looked away, tears in her eyes and a moan half caught in her throat. She leaned against Meredoch, whose eyes were dry and locked to the distance. He rubbed her back absently and murmured soothing words.

"How did you say your father received these injuries?"

Meredoch didn't answer. How could he? What he saw was impossible. All the same, much to his surprise, he found himself answering at length. "A boggart. He said a boggart did this to him."

Lydia looked up at him, eyes reddened and filled with confusion. "What?" she croaked.

55

"It's insane, but I saw something." Meredoch launched into a full retelling, gradually emerging from numbness. He realized he must sound mad.

Lydia regarded him with a cool reservation.

When he finished, Edward spoke. "That seems incredible, but not impossible. You aren't the first to bring us such a tale."

"What do you mean? There's no such thing as boggarts!" Lydia shook her head and leaned away from Meredoch. Her eyes burned with annoyance.

Holding up a hand, Edward replied, "Believe what you will, but this is not the first story of an attack I've heard since moving here. Folks raised in Vogteremark usually know them better as trolls. Since you know what a boggart is, I'd wager you're both from much farther north."

Meredoch splayed his hands. "We were born in the north. Yes. There were only tales there to frighten children, though."

"I didn't believe in them at first either, but if you have a better explanation for why your father looks like a battering ram hit him, I will hear it."

Frowning Lydia said, "Bandits or whoever he was meeting or ..." Her eyes turned toward Meredoch, and though she didn't say it, there was an accusation there that neither could deny.

Clearing his throat, Edward shook his head. "No. I don't believe normal men did this. As I said, I've seen all manner of typical injuries. They look nothing like this.

"Though, trolls do not usually waste their effort maligning every passerby. They carry specific grudges and seek specific gains." Edward stared hard at Meredoch.

With a sigh, Meredoch leaned forward, "You can tell no one of this, but my father was trying to sell the Signet of Thanes. It's the most important—"

"I know what that is," Edward replied, aghast. "How did he

come to possess—your father is *the* Augustine MacCowell? Defender of the Realm?"

"Former, but yes," Meredoch replied. He hung his head in shame. "It's been many years since he forsook that title."

"You mean since the Ords stole it from him," spat Lydia.

Meredoch had never witnessed such hot anger from his sister. He never knew she carried the same grudge, the same animosity he did. She hid it so much better.

"Did the troll speak? I mean, did it say anything of its plans for the ring?"

"It said some Ords wanted the signet." Meredoch shrugged.

"Did it say when the meeting would take place?"

"No. Nothing about that or where."

Edward leaned back in his chair and rubbed his chubby chin. "If you could find his lair during the day, you might be able to retrieve the ring."

"And why is that? It only struck my father twice and almost killed him."

A shudder ran through Lydia, and Meredoch reached for her hand to squeeze it. She jerked hers away.

"Trolls are supposed to be nocturnal. Not sure why. Some say they turn to stone in sunlight, others say it blinds them. Either way, if they hold true, you could get the ring and escape with the beast none the wiser."

"Wouldn't it go looking for the ring?"

"No. Trolls, boggarts, whatever name you give them, are notoriously lazy. Though they have a good sense of smell, so if he ever stumbles on your path, he will probably remember and throttle you. They bear grudges with tenacity."

"And how do you know all this again?"

"Live in this region long enough, and you will hear all sorts of things people take for myths now."

Meredoch mulled this over and remembered Sir Omelek's

words. Gnawing on his bottom lip, he said, "Maybe it is for the best. If I had the ring now, I would return it to the Ords and be done with it myself."

"Who did father want to sell it to?" Lydia spoke up. Meredoch looked at her. Her eyes were hard, and she looked like their mother at her most cross.

"He said the troll promised to sell it to someone in Ecthelowall. Though who, I can't imagine."

"Whomever it is among Ecthels or Ords, you can be sure of one thing," Edward began, "they are familiar with the dark things of this world and will do anything to get what they're after."

"In other words, they are the last people we would want to get hold of the ring," Meredoch surmised, rubbing his temples. "Fine. So, we have to get it back."

Shaking his head, Edward replied, "That, I'm afraid it is your province, Sir Knight. If you haven't noticed, it has been some years since I was battle-ready. Though I can't speak for the lady."

"I need to stay with Father. Any moment could be ... I can't leave. Meredoch, *you* must get it back."

"Very well," Meredoch resolved. "Can you tell me anything more about boggarts, Mr. Goodby?"

"They have tough hides, so look for soft points if you come to blows. But don't let it come to that, because most stories come from others like you. Those smart or lucky enough to watch from a distance."

Pushing back his chair, Edward added, "I'll go check on your father. And you best be on your way, Sir Meredoch. Remember, you have to catch him in the day or not at all."

"Thank you for everything." Meredoch stood and gave a shallow bow.

Edward just doffed his cap and looked at Lydia. "Care to

come and see him again, young lady? It won't be pleasant, but it sounds like you want to be close."

Lydia nodded. Following Goodby, she didn't even glance back at Meredoch when he called to her. "I love you. I'll be back straightaway."

And for that searing pain, Meredoch resolved the boggart would pay.

10

Meredoch crept into the glade, looking left and right. It seemed an impossibly welcome twist that everything led him back here. After days of stalking the boggart, he found himself in the same meadow where it crushed his father.

Across the open space from Meredoch sat the incongruous lump that looked like a moss-covered stone, but he knew it was a malevolent beast of myth. He took each step with great care and watched for any sign that the monster sensed his presence. His pulse quickened.

About five feet away, a sound startled him. He dove and rolled to the side. His hand grasped the hilt of his Spiritsword. The creature. The sound came from the creature.

It's snoring! I suppose they sleep all day and prowl at night.

Meredoch glanced at the sky. The sun perched perilously close to the horizon, but he had no choice. He had to risk it.

He took a steadying breath and edged closer. Meredoch left his horse in the tall grasses. The animal refused to come any nearer. If something went wrong, a quick escape was unlikely. However, the creature had seemed slow before.

He crept right in front of the thing and strained to see the slightest of tremors running through its bulk. Licking his dry lips, Meredoch scanned the contours of its hide. The thing looked largely uniform with some jagged irregularities that must have been bony protrusions on its carapace.

How do I get to its hands?

Lifting his helmet's faceplate, Meredoch wiped the sweat from his face. He circled the creature for ten minutes, looking for some chink in its hide. He found none. Meredoch backed up several paces and put his hands behind his head. He sighed.

I have to pull its arm free.

Surely that would wake the creature, but he *had* to get the ring. Pulling down the faceplate again, Meredoch rolled his shoulders. Feeling the pop, he took one step forward.

"This way!" A voice called from beyond the forested knoll. "We 'ave to hurry. It's almost twilight!"

Meredoch dashed across the grassy expanse and ducked behind a large tree near the clearing's perimeter.

Seconds later, another voice spoke, this one from within the clearing. "No worries. The beast is right here. Still dozing."

"All too easy," a third speaker stated.

"Enough of that," the first said. "Let's kill the thing, take the ring, and be on our way."

Meredoch peered around the trunk. Three Ords stood in the clearing, each in dark garb with hoods pulled overhead.

His buyers!

Taking positions around the creature, they coordinated their moves in silence, until the first speaker called out, "Now!"

In unison, they drew and slammed Ord-sized war hammers on top of the creature's hide. A strange sound followed, not quite of metal on stone.

"Again." The same sound echoed in the clearing.

"Keep at it."

The hammers came down again and again. A cracking sound thundered. "There we go, lads. We have it now!" The cracking sound, unrelated to the hammer strikes, continued and grew louder. Standing at the ready, hammers pulled over their shoulders, the Ords waited. The creature stirred and sounded like a man woken from a deep slumber.

At least as much like a man as the boggart could sound. The beast stretched, and the dwarves moved away, stumbling over their hammers.

"Well, what do we ..." the boggart yawned, "have here?"

"We are Elder Ulster's emissaries sent to complete the transaction for the Signet of Thanes, as arranged," the lead Ord announced.

"Complete the trans ... what?"

"The transaction," the Ord repeated.

"Huh?"

"We're here to retrieve the ring and bring you payment." The Ord sounded unsure himself now.

"Oh, yes. You want the ring. Good. Good. Where's my gold?"

Meredoch gaped. Clearly, boggarts weren't very cunning.

"The gold is near. First, we need to see the ring."

"Ah." The boggart reached into what looked like a collection of hanging moss.

A sack. The peculiarity forced Meredoch to focus on the creature. In the waning light, he noticed its face. Bull-like but still mannish. Moss covered the creature, from its tangled beard to its sharp-boned knees. Though Meredoch couldn't be sure the moss wasn't old garments, rotting away. Two tiny skulls dangled from its beard. *Probably from rats.* A patchwork of rocky looking plates covered its body. Meredoch guessed these were some sort of scale or boney protection. A messy shock of hair topped its head. The monster combed its ape-like hands through it.

"I seem to have misplaced it. If you leave the gold, I can have it for you tomorrow." The boggart produced a wicked grin.

"Ha! You jest," chuckled one of the Ords. "No one told us boggarts had a sense of humor."

"Wirgerd does not jest. He demands!" bellowed the beast. The boggart pointed toward the hammers. "What are these?"

"We weren't sure how to rouse you," the lead Ord replied. His grip on his hammer tightened. "Our master bade us hurry back with his prize. You can see why we needed to wake you early and why we cannot wait till the morrow."

Meredoch knew the Ord was lying, but the boggart seemed unsure.

Flustered, he snapped, "Very well. Bring me my gold and the ring is yours. Be quick about it."

"The ring?" the lead Ord insisted.

"The gold!" The monster stomped a huge foot, sending a faint tremor through the ground.

"Very well. Fulmer, retrieve the chest." The far-right Ord trudged off, and the lead Ord spoke again. "Did you take care of your fence as requested?"

"Ha! That washed-up drunk? Of course. Two swipes, and he died not fifteen feet from where you stand."

Another cruel grin punctuated the beast's words. Meredoch gripped the hilt of his Spiritsword, ready to rush out. Before he moved, the lead Ord asked, "What did you do with his body? Washed up or not, he can't be tied to this."

The boggart leaned back on its haunches. "Birds must have taken him. The body was gone when I got back last night."

"You fool! Is your brain stone as well? Someone must have

seen you." The little Ord leader snapped and slammed his hammer on the ground.

"Maybe, but—" Wirgerd began.

The Ord waved a hand and snapped, "Quiet. You have said enough."

Fulmer returned, dragging a chest.

"Give me the ring and take your gold before you ruin things further."

Wirgerd looked from the Ord to the chest and back a couple of times. A deep, belly laugh rumbled from his gaping mouth. "You think I'm the fool, dwarf? Let me tell you what is about to happen.

"I'm going to smash your puny Ord friends like ants while you watch, and then I'm going to squeeze the life out of you. When I'm done, I'm going to take your gold and have a holiday. Then, I will sell this trinket to the Ecthels for twice the price. How's that for a fool?"

Fulmer shook noticeably, but the leader just snarled. "We shall see, beast. Lads, to battle!"

In unison, all three Ords slung their war hammers at the troll. As Wirgerd raised arms to protect his face, all three hammers dropped to the ground with a thud. The Ords converged on him. Each drew long dirks and leaped on him, jabbing the blades over and over into whatever place they could find. Most stabs glanced harmlessly off the troll's stone plates, but a precious few found their mark on the soft spots between the hard hide.

Wirgerd squalled and grabbed at each Ord. The troll sent Fulmer flying, and he landed with a tumble.

Meredoch watched the resilient Ord stumble back to his feet and hobble back to the fray. The Ord closest to Meredoch wasn't so fortunate. When Wirgerd grabbed him, Meredoch heard a crunch and watched in horror as the boggart launched his tremulous little body into the trees, landing nearby.

Eyes wide, Meredoch covered his mouth to fight a cry of terror. He was witnessing a purer vein of evil than any he had seen in his life.

He missed what happened to Fulmer ultimately, but when he looked up, the troll gripped the Ord leader firmly between two great hands, pinning the Ord's arms at his side.

Wirgerd laughed again, a heinous sound. "Now, didn't I say this would happen, little fool? Greet death for me."

Then he squeezed. The Ord screamed in agony. How long it lasted, Meredoch couldn't be sure, but long enough to be clearly torture. Long enough for his fear and revulsion and panic that froze him to melt in a fiery zeal he'd vowed for others.

In one fluid movement, Meredoch gripped his Spiritsword, unsheathed it, and stepped forward. He may be marching into death's maw, but this cruelty could not continue. No one, Ord, Ecthel, or anyone else, deserved such a fate.

"Drop the Ord, boggart." He felt the heat of his sword's flames swell, heard its familiar crackle turn to the whisper of the High King's words. Powerful words.

The boggart almost did as instructed, looking startled by the incursion. After a moment, he collected himself and sneered. "A bitty knight to join the fray, aye? Why not? It's been too long since I killed a true knight."

The beast couldn't know how that dig wounded Meredoch. Momentarily, his focus wavered, and the sword's flames diminished.

The creature chortled. "Having second thoughts? You should. You know boggarts devour those they loathe most. This Ord is a pest. But you, an intruder. A patsy of that fable-king's cult. You will make for more delicious fare."

Determination surged through Meredoch. Those words enabled him to cut through his personal bitterness. This thing stood in opposition to the High King, mocked all he decreed. If Meredoch let bitterness and shame hobble him, how was he any better than Despero?

Before the rush of heat hit him, Meredoch saw the flare of light surround him.

The boggart stumbled and dropped the Ord. Before Wirgerd could set his footing, Meredoch charged.

Faster than a falcon, ferocious like a lion, he leaped the last seven strides between himself and the beast. Whipping his shield around, he smashed it into the monster's face.

Wirgerd reeled and grabbed his nose. "You broke it you—"

Whatever curses he muttered were lost to Meredoch, who was on him, swinging his sword round in a furious dance that the boggart was surprisingly agile enough to dodge.

In the end, he clipped a huge forearm with his sword tip and found that though his sword didn't cut all the way, it left a deep scorch in what had seemed an impenetrable hide.

Lashing out in surprise more than tact, the boggart caught Meredoch in his distraction and sent him sailing back several feet. The crash didn't hurt as much as Meredoch expected, but it did enough.

He scrambled to his feet. A quick glance revealed Fulmer's remains. Meredoch grimaced. Averting his eyes, he caught the motion in time to see the boggart bearing down on him.

Meredoch threw up a block as another club-like arm swiped at him. This time he didn't fly backward. Giving only a few inches of skidded up soil, Meredoch pushed back. He pushed with all his might and found the troll's face screwed up in unexpected effort.

Digging in, Meredoch pushed but couldn't budge the monster. Each battler strained for several seconds longer, until

Meredoch spun off the contest of wills, and in the spin, sliced at the creature.

The sword struck its leg.

A cry, more awful and blasphemy-filled than Meredoch would ever dare repeat, issued from the boggart's cruel mouth. It grasped its leg. A dark slick ran down. Smoke roiled from the wound.

Meredoch stepped back and drew in a calming breath. He watched the monster coolly.

It returned his gaze. Fear and realization registered in its eyes. Wirgerd might lose this fight. The beast turned and ran, swiping at Meredoch with his jagged tail.

Meredoch almost dodged it, but he caught the hard blow and went down.

The creature didn't even notice. Wirgerd's only concern must have been escape, which Meredoch could not allow.

Wincing, Meredoch got to his feet and ran. He coaxed his legs, urging them to move faster. Another swish of the dangerous tail swiped toward him. He risked jumping onto the troll's back.

Wirgerd flailed, almost knocking Meredoch off. The beast's plates gave Meredoch a place to hang on and leverage a swing to the front of the creature.

As he passed in front of Wirgerd, he went for a deep cut just as the beast bashed him aside.

Meredoch landed face down on the cool grass. Everything hurt. He raised his head. Dizziness dazed him.

Not good.

Against all bodily protests, Meredoch rolled over, expecting to see the boggart coming at him.

Nothing happened. Meredoch looked for Wirgerd but couldn't find him. Then, he saw the beast, balled up on the ground and whimpering. Smoke roiled from his wounds.

Is he trying to go dormant again?

Fighting to his feet, Meredoch forced himself toward Wirgerd.

With each pain-filled step, Meredoch convinced himself the thing must believe him dead or disabled. It did not attempt to retreat, even when Meredoch moved into its line of sight.

Standing only a foot or two away from the creature, Meredoch wondered if it had curled upon itself to die as some animals do. Something felt wrong. The chill on the air still lingered, and that foul smell born by the beast choked him.

Then, as sudden as a cobra strike, the boggart reared up, ripped a jagged shard off its shoulder, and stabbed Meredoch.

The force of the attack brought Meredoch to his knees. The blow hit his helm and could have broken his neck at a different angle. Bits of the stone plating crumbled to the ground in front of him.

"Why don't you die?" screeched the troll. It slammed its fist down like a toddler.

The tantrum helped shake Meredoch to his feet. He fought through muddled and hazy thoughts, forcing himself upright.

"Oh, I see," the boggart said, smug again. "A tough guy, hmm? Like a turtle. Just gotta crack you open."

Meredoch watched as the monster pulled loose his other shoulder shard and reared back to jab it into the armor over Meredoch's breastbone.

Fighting for a tether on reason, Meredoch whispered, "Help me, Great King."

A voice filled his ear, clearer than ever in his life. Meredoch dropped. Less than a second's space separated the shard's swipe and Meredoch's deliverance. With all his remaining might, Meredoch sprang forward and plunged his sword into the troll's soft underbelly. Fire swelled, charring the area around the sword's hilt.

Meredoch thought he should leave it, but the voice insisted he push off, so he did.

A good thing, as Wirgerd's massive bulk collapsed to the ground and sent a quiver through the ground around Meredoch.

Breathing in heavily, greedy for fresh air, Meredoch thought he was going into shock. He rose to his feet, stumbled, and went down a few feet away.

The Ord nearest him wheezed, and his eyes fluttered open. Meredoch reached for his sword, but saw the dwarf barely held onto consciousness. The Ord's eyes, one nearly swollen shut, found their way to Meredoch and widened. "Is that beast gone?" he sputtered.

"Felled, yes," Meredoch replied.

"Then I am next, I suppose. Make it quick." His voice hitched at the end as a spasm of pain must have gripped him.

"I'm not going to kill you, Ord."

"I don't believe you."

Shrugging, despite the tremendous pain the movement carried with it, Meredoch staggered over to Wirgerd's still form. With as much nonchalance as a man picking a violet, he snagged the Signet. Placing it in a pouch, he stuffed it behind his cuirass. "Fine. Believe me or not. I will not harm you."

"Then what are you going to do with me?"

"What is your name?"

"I am Barwnig Feingohl under the banner of Elder Ulster."

Of course, Elder Ulster ...

"Well, Feingohl, I'm going to take you to your home."

PART III

MENDING THE BROKEN

11

Meredoch awoke in a dungeon and scrambled to his feet. His heart thrummed in his chest, his breath caught. Then, he remembered. The trip. Being led down here. Little wonder he panicked. These were the dungeons of what was now called Castle Valesgard. A place with which he was all too familiar.

For a couple of minutes, he sat, taking measured breaths, fighting for calm. Unbidden, the events of the past days returned to him, belaboring his calming exercise.

Twisting his wrists, Meredoch examined the chains that bound him. He squinted in the low light offered by his armor's fiery aura. Heavy rust coated the chains. It amused him that the Ords felt him dangerous enough to merit chaining, but not so much as to take his armor.

From above, a creaking sound issued, and a wan beam of light pierced the gloom. A figure, short and stocky by the silhouette, appeared in the doorway. The new arrival carried a torch and descended the incongruous stairs slowly and awkwardly. Meredoch closed his eyes until the visitor reached the bars of his cage.

Breathing in a heavy rasp, the man spoke. "Wake up!"

"I wasn't sleeping," Meredoch corrected, opening his eyes.

"Smart tongue still in your mouth, I see. Do you remember me, hungerman?"

Meredoch bristled at the use of the slur. When he was first taken captive, the guards had used it so often, he asked after its origin and immediately regretted his query. They were all too happy to inform him it arose from the starvation of hundreds during a siege—the siege that resulted from his father's failed negotiations. All the blame for Thane Denhard's death and the suffering afterward, fell on the Knights of Light, and particularly on Sir Augustine.

"You are hardly worth remembering, Elder Ulster."

"Sadly, your family is impossible for my people to forget. Your father's foolishness brought us to our darkest hour."

Meredoch smirked. "Hmm. I thought it is taught, 'There has been nor will be a darker hour than that which befell Thane Ordumair. From that darkest hour, the greatest triumph of the Ords shown forth.' I suppose there is none meet to the task of restoring Ordumair to a semblance of its former glory."

"You learned your lessons well. So well that I'm sure the value of the Signet of Thanes is not lost on you. That makes the treachery of stealing it all the more profound."

Meredoch's jaw clenched. "How could you know it was stolen? From what I've heard, you Ords have been locked up here since I left."

Ulster's eyes narrowed. "You should know there are ways around our Thane's decrees. You brought Feingohl back to us after all."

"Back to you, you mean?"

Splaying his hands wide, Elder Ulster shrugged. "I do find his tales interesting."

"And I find that you are on cordial terms with monsters *interesting*."

Letting his voice drop to a darker register, the elder said, "Where is the signet? I know that old fool Orwald gave it to you."

"My father took it, didn't he? Then the boggart took it from him. I'm sure whether you admit to employing Feingohl or not, he told you as much. By the way, from what I've heard, you have soiled hands yourself. Your greed for that ring cost two of your own their lives."

Ulster appraised the bars again. "Very well. You and your smart tongue can stay here till you deduce the signet's location. In four days, I will return to check. I would hurry, though. Something about this dungeon has a way of wearing a man down. Most don't live long, and you won't be missed."

Meredoch considered snapping back something equally clever and cutting, but his true revenge would not be in entering a game of taunts with the old usurper. For Meredoch's plan to succeed, Elder Ulster must first leave.

A scowl still etched into Ulster's lined face, he hobbled back to the stairs and out of the cavern. Feigning disinterest in the departure, Meredoch felt a tightness in his chest relax when the door slammed shut.

He drew in a deep breath and waited a full fifteen minutes before moving. It took another fifteen to prepare himself mentally.

Meredoch walked to a jagged outcropping on the cell wall. At one time, it may have been a slab for the cell's bed. Cocking his head to the side, he wrapped his chains around it. In a whisper, he recited, "Stronger than bonds of iron is the steadfast favor of the High King," and yanked with all the might he could muster. The chains clanked against the rock. They resisted, but after a few seconds of persistence, the rusted links shattered.

He huffed in and out after the exertion. The break lasted just long enough to catch his breath, and then he careened, shoulder first, into his cage's gate. Smashing once, twice, the third time the door broke free of its rusted hinges. Meredoch crashed down with it, and he knew from the impact, he would later feel it.

There wasn't time to linger nursing his hurts. His ears still rang with the great sound of the iron's collapse. Others would have heard. On his feet in another heartbeat's space, he dashed toward the far wall.

Meredoch skidded to a stop beside the stone stairs. His fingers hungrily churned through the loose stones. A smirk spread on his lips. He found the secret lever—a quick pattern of clops issued from above. Someone was coming. Not running, but moving with purpose. He had to move fast. In a few seconds, the door would open and thwart his escape.

He yanked on the lever, leaped forward at the cavern wall before him, and landed with a clang inside a dim corridor. Immediately, a familiar musty odor greeted him—the *secret passage.*

Scrambling farther into the tight tunnel, the door he had come through collapsed behind him. He doubted the guards would find the entrance. The dark and confusion of his absence would buy him some time. Regardless, Meredoch needed to keep moving. Getting into the tunnels was the easy part.

Darkness swallowed him as he pressed deeper into the ancient passageways. If memory served him, the tunnel had lanterns and torches lit at intervals. None were lit now, and a layer of collected dust suggested these particular corridors had remained untrod for some time. The air was heavy with neglect and memories past. Meredoch certainly remembered the last time he passed through them. He had been fleeing for his life then. Now his greatest fear was getting lost.

Unlike some myths from childhood, he knew no magic talismans were here. One thing about the Ords might save him from being lost to the tunnels forever.

Meredoch strode down the hall, determined. In front of every passage, he paused.

One. Two. Three offshoots passed.

When he came to the fourth, he took it without stopping. He repeated the pattern again and again. Ulster reminded him, Ords were obsessed with the number four. Ordumair was said to have climbed Mount Fiorsruthain in four days. Four generations passed from their founding to their greatest ruler, Ordumair II. Some particularly zealous Ords claimed they would win the war against the Ecthels in the four hundredth year of its continuance.

With every successive set of four passages, the distances between them increased. All the same, too soon, Meredoch reached the crucial last corridor. He took the fourth juncture's fourth passage. If he was right in his assessment of the Ords, this path led into Ordumair itself, the great fortress and city of his childhood. Started by a man drowning in grief, swollen to inconceivable size by a mad man, and now shepherded by the Ord who had been his closest boyhood friend.

"Well, Duncoin, I hope you're open to a visit."

12

Striding forward, Meredoch brushed aside a series of cobwebs. By the time his father and mother came to live among the Ords, these tunnels were already held as legends. Rumors from his youth invaded his thoughts, stirring up irrational fears. Some said giant rats and spiders crawled along the corridors. Others, and far more of them, whispered the dead Thanes of the past haunted these halls, passing through and exacting terrible suffering upon those who entered unworthily. Foolishness, he knew. But the company of the chill and moldering odor along with the dense darkness worked at every idle imagining. Meredoch almost cried out in spite of himself when his footfall didn't land on solid ground as expected.

Meredoch stumbled. The stony path rushed to meet him much sooner than expected. He caught himself, his armor clanking from impact. The sound echoed with an odd distortion. Meredoch looked up and grinned. The floor sloped up sharply. He stood at the base of a passage leading up into Ordumair.

The rule of four brought Meredoch to Ordumair, but he suspected it wouldn't put him where he ultimately needed to be—the Thane's personal quarters. More than a century of rule by paranoid thanes made those rooms a closely held secret. Most Ords probably believed the Thane dwelled in the keep atop the fortress. It was certainly the most lavish construct in Ordumair. The most important matters of state occurred there. Forbidden from outsiders even before his family's exile, it had only one entrance, two wide doors accessed from atop the Great Bulwark. In short, an impossible goal.

But Meredoch knew something only the Thane and his family were privileged to know. They did not reside in the keep. A series of secret rooms lay deep within the fortress. Duncoin had told him as much.

Unfortunately, his friend never revealed the location. But Meredoch knew someone who would. Someone who owed him at least an audience with the Thane.

The passage Meredoch took leveled, and he found himself beside another of its secret entrances. This time, to somewhere within the fortress. Pressing his ear against the dusty surface, Meredoch listened. He heard nothing. Either the stone was too thick, or no one was on the other side. He drew in a calming breath and gambled on the latter.

Opening the door took some strength, but to his pleasure, he made much less sound than expected. It brought back a memory of an old rhyme he'd heard,

> "Haint in walls of sure stone,
> Hidden doors for Thanes alone.
> Watching o'er little Ords asleep,
> Passing through walls without a peep.
> Ordumair's care for subjects shown,
> Never wavering after grown."

It was the creepy sort of nursery fare told by adults in cheek. Few believed the tunnels were real. Certainly, the residence Meredoch stumbled upon was unaware such a portal existed within their living space. By the High King's grace, it was night still. None of the Ords living in the modest home were aware of his presence.

Taking careful footsteps across the stone floors, Meredoch dared not even breathe. At his right, the room for the adults was open, lacking even a door. A burly Ord lay with one arm lolling out of bed into the floor. His hand held a dagger. Soldiers in the Ord armies were taught to sleep that way. To be ready to spring awake and fight at a moment's notice.

Meredoch swallowed. It felt difficult and sounded painfully loud to him. *I'm not going to be noiseless in this armor anyway.*

Poor comfort, but no one stirred. He took two more steps. Still no signs of interest from the sleepers. Relaxing, he took another step and immediately tripped over a hobby horse left out.

His knees and hands smashed into the floor with a sort of crunch. From the other room, he heard a woman call out, "What was that?"

Meredoch froze and listened. He held his breath, and his heart raced in circles over what to do.

"Dear, dear," the voice continued.

There was a grumbled, not quite coherent, acknowledgment.

"Did you hear that?"

Ord soldiers were taught to be as stealthy as a shadow. The Battle of Landbridge in Ordumair I's day was a victory for it. Tiny Ords snuck up on the Ecthel defenses bearing daggers that cut too quickly and quietly to stop. Meredoch stopped a few steps from the door outside. New worries abounded beyond it. *Waiting here to get carved up by a stealthy dagger isn't better.*

He charged the last few steps and threw open the door to the home. Shutting it behind him, he dashed down an alley. He caught a glimpse of the burly Ord exploding from his home, dagger held aloft.

The soldier looked in each direction but didn't spot Meredoch. Scratching his head, the Ord mumbled something and returned to his house. Meredoch closed his eyes and exhaled. Now that he was out in the open, he must be twice the wraith.

Meredoch glanced around him. Memories muddled his intentions. Despite the risk, he took in one lasting look. This town shaped his childhood. The only place that thrummed with the heartbeat of home.

He drifted into the street, captivated by the sensation of belonging. Every stone welcomed his footfalls as though they had been cut and laid for him.

The city looked utterly unchanged since he left. This round, twenty-one if he remembered rightly, housed the wealthy merchants. The wealthiest Ords and nobles dwelled in rounds twenty-five to the final, twenty-eight. As a child, Meredoch took everything at face value. Now, he would gag on the disparate opulence of the last four rounds compared to those Ords of the lowest rounds.

A few rounds lower, things weren't so difficult to accept. Meredoch kept to the shadows, slipping from street to street until he reached the spot he sought. Checking for signs of others, he stepped from behind his cover.

About a dozen yards away, he saw a crack in the round's flooring. A freak rockslide during the city's construction created the flaw. It only affected rounds fourteen and fifteen, but every round below and above had been redone to make the gap, about eight feet at its widest, look intentional. Duncoin and Meredoch used to peer down from round twenty-six. Every level lit and adorned the crevice in distinctive ways—a prideful competition.

Round seventeen was particularly special. Lattice decorated the crevice and vining plants wrapped around it, growing from troughs along the edge. The round's decorations protruded eight feet above and eight feet below the thickness of the floor. It was magnificent. Meredoch missed few things about his old life—missed enough to admit at least. This was one. Before he moved on, he wanted one last look.

Meredoch approached the crevice. Nothing had changed. In some fundamental way, it felt good seeing the blue clematis still thriving and producing its rich cobalt blooms.

Long windows lined the lattice on each side, spaced about four feet apart, running the sixteen or so feet of the gash. Meredoch leaned to look through one.

"You! Hold right there," a gravelly voice ordered.

13

Meredoch half-turned. A broad-shouldered Ord who came up to Meredoch's chest stood a few feet away. His halberd's point was much closer. Though Meredoch couldn't say for sure, he guessed the man to be the Ord he'd woken earlier.

"No need for hostilities." Meredoch forced a good-natured smile onto his lips.

"Quiet you. I don't know how you got to be in our city, but I'll be hearing that tale after you're in irons."

Brows knitting, Meredoch pushed down his frustrated thoughts and annoyance to find a solution. "Listen, I just—"

"Quiet," the Ord hissed, managing to both keep his voice low and make his tone hit Meredoch like a blow all the same.

Facing away from the Ord, Meredoch held up his hands as if in surrender. Shooting furtive glances around, he searched for some way to escape. He found nothing, just the gaping hole in front of him and its decorative vines.

Meredoch gritted his teeth. A bad plan formed. No, an abysmal plan. That was all he had, though.

"Turn about you fool!" the Ord snapped.

Ignoring the command, Meredoch hopped over the low stone rail circling the round's crevice.

"Hey, you!" The guard snarled and jabbed his halberd forward.

Dodging left, Meredoch used the extra foot or two of distance the hop gave him to grab the halberd's pole near its blade and redirect it.

The Ord spun. Meredoch took advantage of the momentary distraction and squeezed through a window in the lattice. Ducking below its top and grabbing fistfuls of vines, his fingers dug into the lattice and held on tight. "Without doubt, my worst idea yet," Meredoch murmured.

It was hard to tell through the lattice, but it looked as though the Ord was frozen where he stood, gaping at him. Given his probable age and the reclusive ways of the Ords, he had likely never seen a Knight of Light. The speed and agility Meredoch displayed was impossible in a suit of standard armor. Meredoch doubted the Ord could see the lines of flame tracing the characters of words, the High King's words, powerful enough to endow the armor and wearer with such skill.

The reprieve was short-lived. Meredoch shifted along the lattice as the Ord rushed over. A second later, the halberd smashed through the lattice an inch from Meredoch's arm. It disappeared through the lattice and reappeared just over his head.

Meredoch couldn't always see the Ord, but the Ord didn't even have to see Meredoch to skewer him. This would never work. Meredoch let go and leaned back just as the halberd jammed through the vines, missing a direct hit to his chest by less than a breath's space. He watched a pair of blue blooms plummet down the crevice.

Over the sound of the blade sliding back through the

ruined sections of lattice and sundered vines, he heard a whisper." Oh..." Meredoch moaned. He dared not say, "No," though he desperately wanted to.

Taking in a breath, Meredoch let go.

He wanted to scream in terror. The sudden jerk made his stomach feel like it was going to land in his throat. He was falling faster than he expected. Those blooms he'd seen drifting so slowly downward were deceptive. Dread hit hard, making his head fuzzy.

A second later, the last piece of lattice passed in front of his face. His fingers grabbed for a hold with ravenous hunger. But his left hand couldn't find purchase and bounced off. His right hand's fingers grazed the lattice. There were only a couple of inches left.

With a worse jerk than the initial drop, he hooked his fingers into the last rows. Pain jolted up Meredoch's arm, and he almost lost hold. Grinding his teeth, he hung there, hoping his grip wouldn't give.

Reaching up with his left hand, Meredoch grasped for a better hold. As soon as he put weight on that section of trellis, it tore away. Heart-hammering, he listened as the faint crack of wood hitting the stone hundreds of feet below disturbed the quiet.

His fingers burned. He knew his hand wouldn't last long. Looking down, he swallowed hard. He'd have to risk a swing to the next floor. There was at least a chance he'd survive that drop.

"Please, my King!" he whispered and swung his legs. Almost immediately, his fingers began slipping free. Meredoch closed his eyes. The lattice breaking and falling would have been a misdirection for the soldier above, but not for long.

"On three, let go," he told himself. "One. Two. Three ..."

That gut-wringing feeling smacked Meredoch again. For an

instant, he wondered if he would feel it if his swing fell too short. Or would the insane velocity and bone-crushing impact be so instantaneous a death he wouldn't even know it?

He opened his eyes in time to see the ground hurtling toward him. Not the ground hundreds of feet below, but that of the next round.

"Roll!"

A dull thud sounded, followed by the clatter of his armor scraping on the stones. Dark stone and hazy light alternated above him. Short bursts of acute pain pinged his body as he tumbled and bounced at least ten feet from his initial landing spot. When he stopped, he lay sprawled and wondered if he had died regardless of his effort.

One by one, whole areas of his body confirmed, at least for now, that he was very much alive. "Ah, ow." Was there anywhere on him that didn't hurt?

Moving was the most impossible and wretched idea, but he had to. By now, the soldier must have realized the chance that Meredoch lay in a crumpled hulk of metal on Ordumair's first round. Meredoch raised to a sitting position and almost rolled back to the floor as dizziness struck him. Somehow, he rose to his feet and moved.

He descended three rounds. There, he waited in the shadows until he confirmed no one followed him. He backtracked and went up, and up, and up. He had business with the very most elite of Ordumair. Though he had only been on this round, twenty-seven, once before, he remembered the location of Sir Orwald's quarters.

"Hope Orwald is in the mood for a guest." Or at least pliable enough to retrieve his nephew, Thane Duncoin. Otherwise, this would all be for nothing.

Before Meredoch was ready emotionally or mentally, he

arrived. Standing in front of Orwald's door, he sized it up and down and frowned.

There was a lock on it. *Ord nobles never locked their residences.* Boldness, security, or simple folly, Meredoch didn't know. Whatever the source, he hadn't planned for this.

Looking around, he made sure no guards or other witnesses were around. He had no picks, and his Spiritsword was confiscated on arrival.

"Great."

Unlike his cell, Meredoch wouldn't be lifting this door off its hinges. And if it was as solid as he remembered, knocking it down would be hard, noisy work at best. More likely, impossible.

Absurd as it seemed, Meredoch rapped lightly on the door. No response. He knocked again and again, getting progressively louder and more emphatic. Soon, each blow echoed in the hall. Meredoch threw his full weight against the door.

Desperation made him rash, but knowing it was desperate made it less foolish, didn't it? He was probably caught anyway at this point.

Meredoch slammed into the door once more, twice, and on the third time, he felt the door give. But he hadn't battered it open. Someone inside was opening it.

14

The door opened, and Meredoch knew something was off. No lamps had been trimmed within, and Orwald was nowhere to be seen. As he stumbled inside, he heard the whisper from before and dropped to the floor in a roll. Something whooshed through the air where his head had been.

Meredoch crouched and leaped deeper into the room.

Metal's whine on stone gave the shrill warning of a weapon. Which meant ...

He jumped to his feet. Too late. An axe swung around and connected with his upper arm. The glancing blow skidded up and slid off his right pauldron. Before Meredoch got to his feet, the axe smashed into the cuirass over his heart.

The blow sent tremors through the rest of his body. But it didn't pierce his armor.

Unsteady, Meredoch deflected the next attack with his forearm's rebrace. Were he wearing more common armor, his arm would have been lost.

"Of course," he muttered. Meredoch was accustomed to

facing more potent weapons. Weapons enchanted with dark energies.

This common axe had no powers to work against his armor. He deflected the next blow with his opposite rebrace.

Amidst the dark, his armor burned brighter, and he caught the stocky form hovering out of arm's reach. The Ord bounced on the balls of his feet, as though sorting him out.

A shoulder charge would end this. Once he knocked the Ord off balance, Meredoch could pin him, and Meredoch's greater size would take over.

Before Meredoch acted, the Ord straightened and dropped his axe. "It seems I'm at a disadvantage. Name yourself, sir. I see you are a servant of the High King of Light, even if you skulk in shadows of night."

A smirk tugged at the corner of Meredoch's mouth despite his heart's pounding. "Elder Orwald, you're as effervescent as ever," Meredoch replied. "It's been too long."

Orwald's frame tensed. He rubbed his beard and trimmed a nearby lamp. Holding it aloft, he peered across the space. "Bah, you know me for good or ill. But who are you?"

Meredoch's muscles tensed. He knew his response was the knife's edge on which everything rested. "My name is Meredoch MacCowell, son of Augustine, Defender of the Northern Realm."

Orwald went rigid and backed against his door, closing it and using it for support. His old, blue eyes grew wide. "You cannot be here! Why would you come back? Do you mean to work mischief against the old man who saved you and your family?"

Meredoch paused before speaking. His throat felt tight, his tongue heavy. "I remember well what you did. That is why I'm here. To deliver a warning and this as a sign of my gratitude and forgiveness."

Meredoch produced the signet and held it toward Orwald. A tight smile tugged at his lips.

"You villain!" Orwald snarled and raised his axe as if to hack off Meredoch's hand. "So, you do mean to murder my family and me?"

Retracting the ring, Meredoch held out his other hand deferentially. "No, no. I bring this to deliver you. All these years, I kept it secret, but it was discovered, and one of your nobles tried to claim it. By force."

Orwald lowered his axe. "Tried to claim it? Who would be bold enough to violate the law and leave Ordumair?"

"Elder Ulster. Or at least Feingohl, a soldier under his house's banner."

The old Ord spat. "If you had said any other among our people, I would have doubted you. But ..." The old Ord sighed. "Bah. Very well. Deliver your message of warning. I will pass it on to the Thane."

"I'm afraid I must insist on giving it to Thane Duncoin personally."

Orwald looked Meredoch over with renewed suspicion.

The old Ord grumbled something under his breath. Still muttering, what Meredoch thought might be curses, he shuffled toward a nondescript wall. Seconds later, a passage opened, and the dwarf ducked inside.

"Where are you going?" Meredoch called after him.

"To get the Thane. Unless you want your efforts to be empty of meaning."

15

An hour passed since Orwald took Meredoch to the Thane's private quarters. He waited in the scullery where the tunnel's secret passage led. As the interval following Orwald's departure lengthened, Meredoch's hopes for a pleasant reunion diminished.

A series of padded footfalls and hushed conversation alerted Meredoch to Orwald and the Thane's approach. Catching light humor in their tones, for the briefest moment, Meredoch held hope.

"I'm sorry to disturb you, your honor," Orwald said just before opening the double doors from scullery to the adjacent banquet hall.

"It was welcome. Caryn hasn't rested soundly in the bed since her seventh month began. This a reprieve."

Meredoch almost stood but remembered those much taller than the average Ord noble were required to remain seated when one entered a room. Hands clasped together, he watched as Duncoin entered. His old friend's eyes fell on him. The Ord's mouth hung open.

Had Duncoin recognized him? A hardness overtook Duncoin's expression, and emptiness filled his eyes. Meredoch knew his old friend most certainly had.

"Meredoch," Duncoin's voice held the icy cool of a winter's night. "This is unexpected." The Thane shot Orwald a searing look. The old Ord stood stiff as stone.

"My apologies for my lack of convention," Meredoch spoke up. "Formalities were never my strength."

"No. They weren't."

A short silence fell, and Meredoch wavered over what to say next. He picked a topic he immediately regretted. "So, you married Caryn?"

Annoyance spread across Duncoin's face, along with something else. Triumph?

"Yes, I did. She is carrying our first child. A happy family to be."

Meredoch swallowed the bitterness creeping up his throat. A friend turned foe knows far too many ways to wound one. He refused to bite after the implicit digs. "You look quite *Thanely,*" he said instead.

More than redirection, the observation held truth. Duncoin was large for an Ord both in height and physicality. He embodied the warrior ruler his people wanted decades ago. A gold bangle bearing an insignia bound the bottom of his bushy chestnut beard. Reminiscent of the ancient Thane's seal, but not identical.

"You look quite like an intruder," Duncoin retorted dryly.

"Do you know why I am here?"

The Thane glanced at Orwald. "I imagine there was some dissembling. My uncle claimed the lost Signet of Thanes has been recovered."

Meredoch shot Orwald a look of his own and noted a tightening around the Ord's aged blue eyes. Gnawing on his lip, Meredoch shrugged. "You would do well to trust your uncle. He spoke the truth."

Duncoin, seating himself, stiffened. A look blanketed his face—the look he wore the day of their duel. The day Meredoch experienced his vision of the High King. Beneath the thick beard and ornate robes, tough skin and taut muscle dwelt that awestruck boy. The boy disappeared, devoured by a furious man Meredoch had never met.

"You have it?" The Thane grumbled, eyes narrowed.

"I do," Meredoch replied. "No thanks to one of your nobles."

Duncoin drummed his fingers against the polished oak table. "Give it to me. Now."

At the periphery of his vision, Meredoch noticed Orwald give a small shake of his head. Enough to show disapproval but not enough to tip off his nephew.

"I cannot do that, my friend."

Jabbing a finger at Meredoch, Duncoin half-rose. "Do not taunt me, Meredoch. We are beyond childish games. Return what your father stole. Now."

Meredoch felt it. His heart sank with the weight of despair, betrayal. He knew the feeling well, but never with Duncoin as its source. The deepest cut had been saved for his friend to inflict.

"Elder Ulster's plan," he murmured. His voice grew louder. "You knew about it, didn't you? Why didn't you stop him?"

Duncoin sat back in his seat and steepled his fingers. "I think it best if you go now, Meredoch. You should not have come back—"

"What empty-handed? Alive?" Meredoch finished his eyes hard.

Duncoin slammed his fist down on the table. "Enough! The truth!" He paused, his lips pursed as if reining in his emotions. "Tell me the truth. Did your father steal the signet?"

Meredoch shot Elder Orwald a glance. The old man gave another discreet headshake.

Taking in a deep breath, Meredoch replied, "Not from your father, no."

Duncoin's eyes narrowed. He caught the insinuation.

"Such arrogance. You break into my home after your father stole my birthright, and now you want to lead me on a merry chase? What exactly are you, Meredoch, that you come here talking so? You aren't Defender of the Realm. I'm certain your father's debauchery destroyed that dream. You were never noble-born or wealthy. Why should I listen to you?"

"Because you were my friend. My brother." Meredoch rose. "I see now why your father sent the ring into safe-keeping. You are not the son of Denhard."

"And you *are* the son of Augustine MacCowell," Duncoin spat back. "Worse, you are Despero's son."

Meredoch glared at Duncoin, his hand drifting to his hip where his sword's pommel should have been. Remembering its absence, he covered the slip by swirling his finger on the heavy table in front of him. Duncoin didn't say it, but Meredoch felt sure the Ords told the boggart to kill his father. Even if Duncoin didn't scheme it, he permitted it. He noticed Duncoin rested a hand on the shortsword at his side. Not a Spiritsword, just an ordinary dwarf's sword.

At first, it seemed a trifling detail, but the longer he stared and thought, the more it mattered. If one's legacy shaped him, succession defined him. Meredoch did not want his to be this. This duel of bitterness and vengefulness. That was Despero's mantle. Just as it was Elder Ulster's for Duncoin. He had chosen poorly, Meredoch would not.

Easing back into his chair slowly, deliberately, he cleared

his throat. "I did not come to quarrel or do battle with you. You were my brother. I want to warn you."

"Warn me? Of what?" Duncoin interrupted. He sneered but kept his weapon sheathed.

"Of Elder Ulster's scheme to recover the Signet of Thanes. I'm sure he convinced you it was for your honor he planned to retrieve it. But if your people were safe, why would your family want it hidden far from here?"

"Your father stole it!"

"That makes no sense. Why steal it and then hide it for decades? Why steal it at all? No, it benefits no one outside Ordumair to possess the ring."

Duncoin straightened, his hand only resting on his sword's pommel. He seemed conflicted.

"Ask Feingohl about Elder Ulster's true intentions."

"Why would Feingohl tell me truth while employed by a *liar*?"

Meredoch considered his response for a moment. "Offer him a place under another elder's standard. An honored one. Is Kern still an exemplary noble?"

"Kern is dead."

"But his son, Ironhold, is even more influential. His are some of the bravest and most skilled warriors we have," Orwald chimed in.

Duncoin shot his uncle a withering look. But after a few seconds, said, "Say I humor you. What gain is there in doing so? It will not get me back my ring. Will it?"

"No, but it may save your life," Meredoch pointed out.

Strumming his fingers on the table again, Duncoin huffed. "It seems I'm at a bit of an impasse. By your admission, my most trusted advisor and mentor will tell me you are evil. You, my one-time-friend, tell me he is evil. It is like the myth of the dual springs, isn't it? One hot, one cold, running side by side. You know, it is said the springs do exist somewhere in this mountain."

"I'm surprised you doubt their existence. They allowed Thane Ordumair to survive long enough to claim the birthright and his throne. You are seated there because of that *myth*."

"If legends be true," Duncoin amended with a shrug.

"Unlike Ordumair, your two springs are not equally for your good. What will the legends say of your choice?"

Duncoin regarded Meredoch coolly for a few seconds. He stood abruptly. "We shall, shan't we? I will investigate this myself.

"You will remain here with my uncle until I do. My personal guard will keep you here, so don't bother attempting escape."

Looking Meredoch over, he added, "As you have no weapon, I suppose you can't be much trouble."

Meredoch chuckled darkly. "If I had come to make trouble, you wouldn't be able to hold me. Don't you remember our duels?"

"Oh, yes, I remember." Duncoin opened the door. "But those days are long gone."

"I never wanted harm for you or your people. And I never got to offer condolences for your father. He was an honorable thane and a good Ord."

"Others tell me he was only a tolerable thane," Duncoin muttered. He lingered by the doorway. "They told me Feingohl captured an outsider and brought him here. I was also told Feingohl could barely move. I will bear all this—and your words—in my decision-making. Do not place your hope in it for a favorable outcome, son of Augustine."

Slamming the door behind him, Thane Duncoin was gone.

"Hmm, so now we wait and see whether you bribed that

Feingohl better than Elder Ulster." Orwald shook his head. "You play long odds, lad. Like your father."

"That's the first time anyone has compared us in a positive way," Meredoch said with another dark chuckle.

"It wasn't a compliment."

"I didn't bribe Feingohl." Meredoch rose to his feet and stretched.

"What? Then how do you expect him to be loyal to the truth?"

"I just know."

Orwald dropped into a chair and rested his head on the table. "If you aimed to kill me, you might have done it in a more civil way."

"Neither of us is going to die." Meredoch patted the old Ord on the back.

Orwald waved Meredoch's hand away. "What convinces you of that?"

"Because I am not my father. But I am his son."

16

Dawn stretched its golden fingers over the last hill separating Meredoch from the gates of Estonbury. Every limb and muscle ached. Hunger racked his stomach, his feet throbbed, and he shook from the effects of exposure. All he wanted was to stop. To rest. Of course, he couldn't do that for the risk of never getting up again. Whether it was his body giving in to the toll of the trip or more likely being found in the night by an Ord blade. Under his ragged breathing, he reminded himself, "Stopping means death."

That knowledge made his final exchange with his childhood friend all the more galling.

'There is some truth in you. In view of this, we grant you your life,' Duncoin had said in dismissal.

'We were like brothers once. I hope for this we might one day be again.'

'Hardly, Sir Meredoch. The only manner in which you may return is to witness my triumph. I will achieve what neither your father nor my ancestors could—lasting peace. On that day, you may stand at my side again.'

What was he supposed to say to that? Nothing regarding the Thane's arrogance would have helped, so he fled. Elder Ulster's treachery had been revealed, but moving against the elder would take more time. One with Ulster's influence and position could not be easily discarded. Which meant anyone who crossed the elder remained in danger.

Meredoch wasn't given any supplies for the trip when he left Ordumair. Not even a tinder box to better start needed fires for warmth in the chilly region. To be safe, he'd kept to the wilds, avoided the nearest city of the Vogteremark, Sorgby. Long ago it had been Aagen, an important town in the Ord's lands. If Ulster had eyes in Estonbury to watch his father's deterioration, then Sorgby was too dangerous.

Meredoch ran over hills and alongside the River Orthall for many miles, pursed by Ulster's men. Even taking the circuitous route and sticking to the wilderness, Meredoch barely outdistanced them. Without his horse or Spiritsword, he could scarcely defend himself. Forage, hide, dash out under cover of night and well into the next day. Over and over.

Cresting the last hill between himself and the sanctuary of Estonbury, Meredoch's heart sank. A group of seven of Ulster's thugs waited outside the smooth, creamy walls of the sprawling city. Or so he guessed. They wore dark cloaks and bore postures of those in wait. *In wait for him.*

"All right then."

Chewing at the mint leaves in his mouth, Meredoch spat them out and downed the last of the blackberries he'd scavenged. If this were going to be his last stand, he would make it count. Whoever felled Sir Meredoch MacCowell would do so only with great struggle.

The open rolling landscape around Estonbury provided no cover. Surely the heptad spotted him. None of them moved to intercept, not even as he closed in the last ten yards. *Had he been wrong about them?*

As if summoned by his thoughts, the cloaked men advanced as one.

Meredoch's measured pace came to an abrupt halt. His short-lived relief coursed away in a rush, leaving him dizzy. He could not win this fight. Armed, unarmed. They had numbers and weren't ravaged by exhaustion and exposure. His fingers fumbled and found the Signet of Thanes. After they murdered him, they would no doubt find it.

The group neared him now.

He pushed down the ring and dropped into a defensive stance. Drinking in the cool evening air, he bolstered himself for the fight of his life, his last. "Take me if you will. But know that my only aim was the Thane's peace."

All seven figures halted. Tall for dwarfs, most probably mercenaries hired by the elder. At least he could die knowing it would cost Elder Ulster a hefty sum to get his revenge.

"Did you leave from Ordumair in peace?" one of the hooded men asked.

What an odd question. Did they not recognize him? "I did. Thane Duncoin knows of Elder Ulster's treachery."

"And the signet?"

"It's safe from those who would misuse it."

"You have it, then?"

"Why bother with more banter? Come and find out."

The speaker turned his head and regarded the others loosely arrayed around Meredoch. Each of them nodded. "That won't be necessary, honored, sir." The man pulled back his hood. "Welcome home, Sir Meredoch, Defender of the Realm."

At first, Meredoch was too on edge to process anything. Tricks wouldn't be needed to finish him. Something appeared familiar about these faces surrounding him. The twilight shadows made it hard to be sure. "Sir Matthias?" he ventured.

"The very same."

A choked sound escaped Meredoch's throat. Forged of a sob and a laugh, an echo of the bitter journey only sweetened by this end. He couldn't be hallucinating all this, could he?

"What are you doing, lurking outside the city gate?"

Sir Matthias, a tall thin man in his late forties, looked like a chastened puppy. "We weren't lurking, sir. We were told to wait outside the walls for your return."

Looking over the assembled group, Meredoch found affirming nods from all: Sir Renaud, Sir Mendelev, Sir Brod, Lady Constance, Lady Talia, and Sir Hector. All reputable Knights for whom waiting outside the city seemed an odd task.

Meredoch took in a couple of deep breaths, his thoughts still fuzzy by his exhaustion. He could only think of one reason for the strange meeting. "Did Sir Omelek prompt you to do this?"

A pleased smile eclipsed Matthias's look of concern. "He did. And both provided your final test and the answers you would give, confirming you are indeed the High King's choice to succeed Sir Augustine."

Gaping, Meredoch remembered Sir Matthias was one of the Knights he had looked up to from his childhood on. "Are you sure of this?"

Meredoch observed the group. Their smiling faces added brick-to-brick on his weight of disbelief. *Was this real? After everything he'd suffered and striven through, had he succeeded?*

"Your father will be very proud, I'm sure," Lady Constance commented. She had always been kind toward his father after his fall.

Not even looking at her, Meredoch muttered, "He's dead."

"What?" Matthias asked.

Constance's hands flew to her mouth. She appeared as though Meredoch had struck her.

"He was mortally wounded by a boggart. I left him in Bracken with Lydia. After facing the creature myself, I returned and found he'd died some hours before I'd made it back. Lydia was gone. She didn't even leave a note."

Meredoch didn't look up. His exhaustion was too deep to let himself feel the sorrow the way he would if he saw their expressions now. He waited, as long seconds of silence stretched to more than a minute.

At last, one of the seven, Sir Percy, cleared his throat. "You say Sir Augustine was killed by a what?"

Facing this was far easier. Meredoch looked up and took in the confusion on Sir Percy's face. The man had never ventured beyond Estonbury's lands.

"A boggart. You call them trolls."

Sir Brod shook his head, "Such things don't exist."

Meredoch considered each of the prestigious Knights of the Hall standing before him. The most highly honored of Estonbury. Yet now, after all he'd experienced, they seemed green. "I need to speak with Sir Omelek. He will understand."

Matthias banged a fist against his leg and cleared his throat. "You should hurry. Sir Omelek took a turn for the worst while you were away. He hasn't long."

All at once, Meredoch's legs gave out. He crumpled to the ground with a clank. The solid stones of the road winding into Estonbury were all that kept him from plummeting forever on. He had lost his father, his sister, his oldest friend, and now his mentor. Meredoch felt so very alone.

"Sir?" Matthias placed a hand on Meredoch's shoulder.

Collapsing like this probably didn't instill tremendous confidence in him as a leader. All the same, it took all his will to respond. "Can you please take me to him?"

"Of course." Matthias helped Meredoch to his feet. "Follow me."

No sound above a hushed whisper encroached upon the Knight Hall. Even so, their collective weight made the room heavy with somberness. Candles burned low, and aromatics mingled with an unpleasant smell.

Central to the gathering stood a bier. Perhaps more conventional bedding than its standard purpose, but given the stillness of the frame's occupant, Meredoch felt his breath catch. *I'm too late.*

A hush fell on the room as he moved toward Sir Omelek. Eyes tracked him, some in surprise, others pleased, still others sorrow-stricken.

Meredoch reached the bedside. Omelek stirred. He shuddered with a vicious, throaty cough. "I see you have returned," he wheezed.

Meredoch swallowed hard. "I have, sir."

"Then you have triumphed. You shall succeed your father as Defender of the Realm."

Waiting until a fresh round of coughing passed, Meredoch replied, quiet, "Are you sure, sir? I didn't accomplish the task you required."

Omelek raised a brow. "Haven't you? Did you travel to Ordumair?"

"I did."

"Were you murdered there? Are you merely a spirit?"

"No, sir. The Thane allowed me to leave."

"Then it would seem I spoke rightly."

Clenching his jaw, Meredoch dug out the signet. "I still have this though."

"You did not offer it?"

"I ... at first. But I couldn't give it to Duncoin in good conscience. Ulster would have assassinated him to get it."

"So, you appeared without invitation and left in peace. How did that happen?"

"Duncoin spoke with me. One of his own corroborated my testimony about the danger from within his people."

"And then you were allowed to leave. Child, I suspect whatever hostility lay between you and Duncoin is buried and forgotten."

"I made peace with one Ord. You sent me to reconcile with them all."

"Did I? I will keep my own counsel as to what I meant by my words."

A scowl etched itself into Meredoch's face. One Omelek somehow saw even with his aged eyes closed.

"You still dispute your selection within. Why?"

"Because I'm too much like my father. I saw the darkness in the world and what it did to him. I can fall just as easily. Maybe more after all I suffered."

"Do you think the High King could've spared you those sufferings?"

"Of course. There is none greater than he."

"Then, you blame him for suffering as you did?"

"No. Not at all. The sufferings ... instructed me—if that makes any sense."

A smile creased Omelek's lips. "You are like your father. But not as you see it. His former strength and compassion dwell in you. You have something more, though. You have seen the darkness of this world in its varied forms—both within and without.

"Your father never faced that darkness, and it overwhelmed him. There is no better choice for a realm so close to tipping into the pit of shadows."

A fierce coughing fit seized Sir Omelek. When at last the

choking subsided, each breath sounded irregular. Like wind through a jagged cavern.

Meredoch looked away.

"I think now I would rather have followed you in your work. Helping people far from here would be marvelous."

"The peoples of this realm are broken, divided. They are hurting. You are well acquainted with this. Sir Meredoch MacCowell, Defender of the Realm, shall face the sinister elements waiting like wolves. Remember ..."

Sir Omelek gasped suddenly. The final words were almost lost on his whisper-thin last breaths.

In the silence that followed, Meredoch tested them aloud. "Once you can see one, you will see them all."

For a long while, Meredoch sat still. He watched as the attendants bound the old Knight Errant's body in sheets and carried him away to prepare for burial. Many in the room came to congratulate and console him. He barely noticed. He thought himself alone when someone cleared his throat behind him. Meredoch snapped out of his daze.

Sir Matthias stood a few feet away. "Did you receive the comfort you needed?"

"Comfort?" Meredoch tried the word. He shook his head and clenched his fists reflexively. "Not comfort. A conferral. I accept the right of succession and will serve the High King."

PART IV

THE GATHERING DARK

17

Year 1605 of the Middle Era

Meredoch eyed his unexpected visitor in the flickering light of the room's candles. Garbed in a rich indigo cloak and ornate silver mail, he wondered how the dwarf got here unaccosted. Perhaps he had been attacked by bandits. He looked like the sort who could handle himself in a scrap. "What brings one Ordumair's fine warriors all the way to Black River's backwaters?"

The Ord snuffled. "Backwaters indeed. A speck. But I obey orders, hungerman." He produced a fresh parchment scroll.

Reaching out, Meredoch grasped the scroll as he would a battle-axe for a duel.

If the Ord noticed his hesitancy, he did not address it. He did speak when Meredoch stared at the indigo wax seal in the parchment. "You're a hard man to find Cinaed of Bracken."

"Cinaed of Black River now," Meredoch corrected absently, as he noted the differences in the seal's image from the genuine signet of Ordumair's thanes.

"Harrumph. Disgraced like all in your order, hmm?"

Meredoch debated explaining the arrangement of his advanced title and decided against it. He was here for humility, service. The nuances would be lost on the Ord anyway. "We all have pasts we flee." He nodded to the single flaw in the Ord's armor. A scratched-out engraving of a family standard—Elder Ulster's.

The stocky Ord's bushy beard pulled back as his lip curled in a sneer. "You more than any you spawn of a ..."

Meredoch broke the seal and unrolled the scroll, ignoring the insults the Ord lobbied against his entire ancestry, Order, and general incompetence. He scanned the letter and took a shaky breath. He should've steeled himself. Meredoch re-read it more slowly, guarded.

Duncoin, son of Denhard, Thane of Ordumair to Meredoch MacCowell, duly appointed Defender of the Northern Realm. Also styled as Cinaed of Bracken, Knight Errant of the Knights of Light:

I write you, old friend, in the best and worst hours of my life. You are a man well acquainted with pain. Elder Ulster is long dead. Hung himself while in the dungeons of Valesgard. He attempted to poison me after your escape. It was not entirely successful. Caryn, by chance—or fate I cannot say—received the tainted portion meant for me. She only had very little, but it sent her into labor. The delivery was long and difficult, the child stillborn, perhaps from the poison. A week later, she died as well. You are the only other person who may grieve as I did and still do.

Not just for Caryn, but for all that has been taken from us. The betrayals and manipulations that robbed both us and those we serve of a better world—one with far more peace and joy.

After our terse parting and years of silence, I will not hold it against you if this letter is met with hostility. My vanity and naiveté have cost me dearly. I have no heir to share the joy of what I am about to write. Only you, with whom I am estranged. You see, dear Meredoch—or Cinaed, whomever you choose to be—the propitious hour of Ordumair's triumph is upon me. Peace with Ecthelowall, at long last, will be realized. We are to have a formal signing of the treaty on Fylleth 28th.

What we long hoped for will come to pass. I would have you by my side and request you leave immediately. A permanent courier for my people is posted in Estonbury, at Arbear's Inn and Tavern. You will find it near the corner of Markeson Way. The courier will bring you to Valesgard. I promise you an amicable welcome.

Do not delay and bring such family or kindreds as you have as equal guests.

~ Duncoin son of Denhard, Thane of Ordumair

"Duncoin wants me to witness the accord?"

The Ord bristled. "The Thane of Ordumair commands your attendance."

"He isn't above gloating..."

Meredoch's comments fell off as he caught a whisper on the air, faint, but resting on his ears like the heat radiating from a nearby fire. He put his hand on the Spiritsword at his hip.

The Ord tensed and went for his weapon.

Realizing his mistake, Meredoch held his sword hand up placatively. Listening for the whisper, he sucked in a shallow breath and blew it out. "I will bring this matter before the Great King once more. Go or stay, I'm sure you will have your answer by this time tomorrow."

A loud clang resounded from the hall. The Ord beside

Meredoch jumped back and drew his sword in one deft move. Without doubt, capable in a scrap.

Meredoch drifted back a step. The whisper from before had carried no warning, and he felt only his heart's increased beating.

Sounds of a hasty retreat. Like a bowstring tensed and then released, the Ord sprang forward. Meredoch followed, and as they entered the hallway, he caught a glimpse of a lanky figure stumbling away.

Who would be here so late? Anargen!

Before he rounded the corner, Meredoch caught the Ord's broad chest and pushed him back, narrowly avoiding a sword swipe as he did.

"What treachery is thahs?" bellowed the Ord, his people's brogue thickening.

"None, I promise. Only harmless curiosity from a local," Meredoch assured, both palms up, but well out of reach.

"There is no such thing." The Ord advanced a step on Meredoch. "My people's blood screams it!"

Meredoch bit back a cruel retort. "It does, and it also demands you heed your Thane. He bade you deliver his message and return."

The Ord's posture shifted from partially directed toward the hall's exit to completely facing Meredoch. The light wasn't sufficient to know, but there seemed to be murder in his eyes. "Hungerman churl! Do not presume to tell me what my people—"

"Ord law demands you address the favored of the Thane with respect," Meredoch boomed, setting the Ord off footing. "My oath is guaranteed by the Thane's honor. Do you dispute your Thane's honor?"

Though he knew his question should have totally disarmed the Ord, Meredoch kept back. It was well he did.

The messenger pointed his short sword at Meredoch's waist and gave a couple of pointed jabs. "You do not speak for my people, hungerman." He muttered something under his breath.

Was he really questioning Duncoin's honor? Such a thing would've been unthinkable in Meredoch's youth.

The Ord still seethed but didn't advance.

Meredoch cleared his throat. "You are right, pardon my indiscretion."

The Ord's eyes narrowed, and his gaze drifted toward the Knight Hall's doorway. Anargen should have been long gone by now, and they both knew it. "Harrumph. Very well. I take my leave." He pointed a thick gauntleted finger at Meredoch and rapped it on his chest. "You will heed the summons, or I will return for the just punishments disparaging a Thane's honor merit."

"As you say it. If you like, I will accompany you to the next town to ensure safe passage."

The Ord laughed, cruel and throaty. "You and your stone-cold spiritblade have no power to assure me, hungerman. I will go as I came—alone."

Meredoch nodded. "Hale night, and may the High King guard your travels." Almost as an afterthought, he added, "You don't know who I am, do you?"

"The successor to a long line of charlatans and brigands. All under the banner of your failed knight order," the Ord replied, his voice icy as the grave.

Meredoch pursed his lips but said nothing. At length, the Ord turned and stomped into the night. Left to himself, Meredoch, gathered some things and drifted into his study.

Pulling a weather-beaten chest from under his table, he undid the padlock. It had been years since he'd opened it. It took a moment to find what he sought amidst things and mementos from faraway lands, but a blue sack corded by a silver thread held what he needed now.

"Once you can see one, you will see them all," he recited, as he regularly had over the years. He dropped the signet into his palm and drew in a deep breath. It was time. Meredoch MacCowell, Defender of the Northern Realm, was returning to Ordumair. The hour of the Ords' succession was at hand.

ABOUT THE AUTHOR

Brett Armstrong, author of the award-winning novel, *Destitutio Quod Remissio*, started writing stories at age nine, penning a tale of revenge and ambition set in the last days of the Aztec Empire. Twenty years later, he still tells stories enriched by his Christian faith and a master's degree in creative writing. His goal with every work is to be like a brush in the Master artist's hand and his hope is the finished composition always reflects the design God had in mind. He writes to engage, immerse, and entertain with deep, thoughtful stories. Continually busy at work with one or more new novels to come, he also enjoys drawing, gardening, and playing with his beautiful wife and son.

You can learn more about Brett by visiting his website: BrettArmstrong.net

ALSO BY BRETT ARMSTRONG

The Gathering Dark:

Quest of Fire Series – Book One

After a thousand years of light, a teen's world teeters on the edge of utter darkness.

Jason is an expert at running from his past. But when it catches up, he finds himself hiding in a peculiar inn listening to a tale from centuries past.

The story is Anargen's, a teen who is pulled from all he loves to follow his oaths of loyalty to the fabled King of the Realms. Together with his mentor, Cinaed, he rides north on a special quest to mediate peace talks between ancient foes—the men of Ecthelowall and the dwarfs of Ordumair. Nothing goes as planned. Many on both sides of the dispute despise Anargen's Order. Worse, an arcane evil has returned to the North. This "Grey Scourge" seeks to ruin the peace talks and ensure a lost treasure held by the dwarfs is never found by those for whom it is meant.

As Anargen's story unfolds, Jason begins to wonder whether it is truly just a fable. He soon finds himself drawn into the conflict Anargen faced. A battle that has shaped and can destroy his world.

The Gathering Dark is a finalist in the 2020 Selah Awards for Speculative Fiction.

North to Chimney Rock, and finally to the Center—and the final confrontation—in Chaco Canyon.

Get your copy here: scrivenings.link/kokopellissong

The Letters

Rachel Hamar—a Manhattan bank teller—lives nothing close to a Manhattan lifestyle. Residing in Washington Heights, NY, the only thing keeping her in The Big Apple is her mother—a long-time patient in a local psychiatric hospital. It's December 2014, and the twentieth anniversary of her high school sweetheart's tragic death. She's not sure how much more heartache she can endure, especially after being told earlier in the day she no longer has a job at the bank. A casualty of downsizing.

In the midst of spiraling depression, Rachel receives a mysterious letter in the mail. When she opens it, she becomes cautious and skeptical of its contents and discards it as a mistake, concluding it's simply addressed incorrectly or a postal worker's faux pas in the midst of a busy Christmas season. But another letter arrives the next day. And another the day after that. Before long, she is in possession of several letters. Each one more puzzling than the last.

Thinking that someone may be playing a cruel game, she contacts the police, and this propels Rachel and the two detectives into one of the most bizarre cases they've ever encountered. Is it a friend's cruel joke? Is it some stalker's perverse idea of manipulation? Or is it something more?

Get your copy here: scrivenings.link/theletters

The Seer

Book One of The Kalila Chronicles

Viktor has one order to follow:

Kill the girl before her eyes are opened.

For thousands of years, his job has been to torment and kill seers: humans that have the gift of seeing the spiritual realm. So it was no surprise when his brother Matthias was once again sent to stop him and protect the girl.

Now the last of the seers' bloodline hangs in the balance, as the estranged demon and angel brothers are forced to work together to save a girl's life and escape to the sanctuary city of Bethesda.

Get your copy here: scrivenings.link/theseer

Stay up-to-date on your favorite books and authors with our free e-newsletters.

ScriveningsPress.com

www.ingramcontent.com/pod-product-compliance
Lightning Source LLC
Chambersburg PA
CBHW070658100726
47907CB00007B/2255